HANNAH AND ⟨...⟩STERS

AN ERIE CANAL ADVENTURE

BY

IRENE UTTENDORFSKY

ILLUSTRATIONS

BY

DANNY J. MILLS

SPRUCE GULCH PRESS

BOX 4347

ROME, NEW YORK
13442

Published by Spruce Gulch Press

Rome, New York

13440

Printed by Instantpublisher.com

ISBN 0-9625714-2-3

FOR REBECCA,

Your journey has just begun

This is a work of fiction. While I have tried to tell my story with historical accuracy, characters are either the product of my imagination or used in an imaginary way.

HANNAH AND THE TWO SISTERS

CHAPTER 1

April 1864

HANNAH'S REVENGE

Hannah pushed back the hood of her blue woolen cloak and listened. Raging torrents of snow melt and spring rain roared between the banks of Mill Creek. Between the noise of the creek and the patter of rain, it should be easy to sneak up on John.

She scanned the near bank, then smiled to herself. He was there all right, standing on the bank of the creek skipping stones across the roily water.

Hannah pulled her cloak tighter against the frosty air. Why did April in Boonville always have to feel like November?

She blew on her hands, her warm breath rising like a plume of smoke in the frigid air. Her shoes were rain-soaked, her feet pins and needles cold. The steady rain had turned her backyard into a wintry swamp.

John whipped another stone across the water.

Tears stung Hannah's eyes. Maybe she should just go back inside. What good would it do, anyway?

She frowned, remembering. He had yanked her braids again this morning, so hard she screeched. And then he laughed and ran away with her books, taunting and teasing. And every time she tried to get them back, he dodged and sprinted away, time and time again.

Hannah clenched her jaw, her cheeks burning as her smoldering anger flared. If she didn't do something he would never stop plaguing her.

She took off on a dead run, her arms out straight, her cloak billowing out like a flag of war.

"Take that, John Henry Nichols," she said, shoving him as hard as she could.

"Hey," John yelled, flying off the bank like he

had been hurled from a catapult. He splashed down and sank like a rock.

Hannah panted, watching for him to come up.

When his head bobbed above the surface he coughed, spewing muddy water from his mouth and nose.

Hannah laughed. She laughed so hard she had to bend over and hold onto her stomach.

"Are you crazy?" John said. He flailed his arms to keep his head above the flooded creek.

"Maybe you'll remember this the next time you decide to pull my braids," Hannah said. She turned to walk away.

"Wait! You can't leave me here… I'll drown!"

Hannah looked back.

"John?"

All she could see was churning froth. She wrung her hands, pacing back and forth on the bank.

"Please don't let him die," she said

CHAPTER 2

THE PITCHFORK

"Thank God," Hannah said when John's head came up again.

"I'll help you if you promise never to pull my braids again," she called to him.

"I swear," John said, grabbing onto a branch. "Hurry!"

The branch broke with a resounding crack.

Hannah drew a sharp breath as the turbulent water dragged him back under. He took longer to come up this time.

Now, she knew she had to get him out . . . before it was too late. Frantic with fear, she looked around for something she could rescue him with.

Pa's pitchfork. He must have left it stuck in the ground near the creek after he cleaned out the horse stall.

Hannah raced to the pitchfork, yanked it out of the soggy ground, then looked back.

John's head bobbled in the riotous water. He must have grabbed onto another branch.

"I'm coming," Hannah said.

Rain pelted her face and dribbled off her nose as she charged across the wet uneven ground. When she neared the creek she paused, pushing her wet hair away from her eyes. There . . . a sturdy tree, close to the creek bank and John.

"You'll have to let go!" she yelled, waving the pitchfork in the air as she ran.

"Why? So you can finish me off?" His voice was thick, his words slurred.

Working feverishly, Hannah wedged the pitchfork against the tree trunk so that the handle stuck out over the water, then, leaning into the curve of the times, she steadied the handle with both hands.

"Let go and grab on!"

"I will, when I get closer," he said, gasping.

Why did he have to be so bullheaded? If he didn't let go right now, he might be too weak to hang on by the time he did.

Hannah frowned, watching John inch himself closer to the bank along a half submerged tree limb.

"Let go!" she screamed, as the limb broke loose and swung downstream.

CHAPTER 3

THE RESCUE

John lunged for the pitchfork handle.

"Oof!" said Hannah, as John's weight and the force of the current snapped the fork tines against her. She dug her heels into the soggy ground and clenched her leg muscles, locking her knees to stop them from buckling.

She willed her wet hands to hold fast to the slippery, water-soaked handle, as little by little she pulled him closer to the bank. His grip on the handle loosened.

"Don't let go," Hannah screamed, when she saw his hands slipping. She grabbed him by one wrist, and, with every ounce of strength she had left, yanked him out of the water, flopping him on the muddy bank like a fish on a hook.

"John," she cried, dropping to her knees, her eyes searching his face.

His teeth clattered like a woodpecker on a dead tree. His thick brown hair was plastered to his forehead, droplets of muddy, creek water clinging to his eyelashes. Except for the bluish shadow that ringed his mouth, his face was colorless.

"Take my cloak," Hannah said, pulling it off and tucking the wet wool around him like a blanket.

John opened his eyes and gave her a foolish grin. "You don't smell so good," he said.

Hannah sniffed the air. Dang! Horse manure. She frowned at the dark brown, telltale streaks that trailed across the front of her apron, then scowled.

"I better get you home," she said, tight-lipped.

John gave her a weak laugh.

Hannah pulled him to his feet, then draped her soggy, smelly cloak around his shoulders. She shivered in the cold rain which was rapidly soaking her to the skin without her cloak. She slid one arm around John's waist and pulled his other arm over her shoulder. He sagged against her, his weight heavier than she expected.

"Your ma will have a conniption fit," she said, struggling across his backyard.

"John," Mrs. Nichols cried, running out to meet them. She threw her arms around him, pulling him away from Hannah.

Hannah's legs were so stiff and numb from the cold that she stumbled and nearly fell.

"How did this happen, John?" his mother asked.

Hannah glanced at Mrs. Nichols, then hung her head. Like a condemned man waits for the hangman, she closed her eyes, waiting for John's answer.

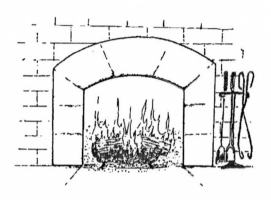

CHAPTER 4

FROZEN CARP AND DROWNED RAT

"I slipped, Ma," John said. "I would have drowned if Hannah hadn't been there."

Hannah's eyes snapped open. She stared at John.

"Thank God you were there, Hannah," said Mrs. Nichols, smiling at her.

Hannah felt worse than she imagined she would have felt if John's mother had publicly horse-whipped her. For a second or two Hannah thought about telling the truth . . . but in a way, it was the truth. If she hadn't been there to pull him out, John probably would have drowned.

"Come in and get warm," Mrs. Nichols said, waving her inside. "I'll send for your ma."

Hannah followed John and his mother to the parlor, where a crackling fire in the marble fireplace radiated a marvelous heat.

Mrs. Nichols wrapped a lap quilt around both their shoulders, then stepped back.

"Why were the two of you out in the pouring rain in the first place?" she asked.

Hannah studied the pattern in the Oriental rug

John said nothing.

"You're fifteen years old, John," his mother said, "and just getting over the grippe as it is."

Hannah stifled a giggle. Mrs. Nichols sounded like an old mother hen, clucking and fussing over her brood.

Mrs. Nichols shifted her gaze to Hannah. "And you're old enough to know better, as well," she said, shaking her head. That said, she whirled and ran from the room.

Hannah looked at John. She giggled. "You look like a frozen carp somebody just hauled out of the canal."

John snorted. "At least I don't look like a drowned rat, or smell like I got drug through a horse stall." He drew his lips up over his front teeth, pinched his nose and made rat noises.

Hannah sniffed the air, then wrinkled her nose. The heat of the fire was ripening the stench of the horse manure on her apron. She stuck out her tongue at him.

John wiggled his nose and bared his teeth again; and all of a sudden it was the funniest thing Hannah had ever seen.

By the time Mrs. Nichols returned, Hannah and John were bent double by peals of laughter.

"I'm glad you're feeling better," she said, frowning, "but I fail to see the humor."

Hannah bit her lip to stop laughing and tried to compose her face in a mournful expression. She didn't dare look at John for fear she would burst out laughing again. But then she glanced out the window and winced.

Ma was coming on a dead run.

CHAPTER 5

A TANGLED WEB

"What on earth happened?" Ma said, looking first at Hannah, then John.

"John Henry fell into Mill Creek. Thank God Hannah was there to pull him out," Mrs. Nichols said, rolling her eyes heavenward.

Ma raised one eyebrow. "Well, I'll be," she said, looking Hannah in the eye.

Hannah cringed, bracing herself for the tongue lashing she knew she deserved. Ma only cocked her eyebrow when Hannah wasn't telling the truth.

But Ma just gave her a questioning look, then turned to John.

"I'm sorry for your trouble, John Henry," she said.

Hannah hung her head and stared at her muddy shoes.

"I better get you home," Ma said, taking her by the arm and propelling her out the door.

"Thanks for saving John," Mrs. Nichols called after her.

Ma pulled the door shut behind her.

"When we get home," she said, her tone ominous, "I expect to hear the truth about how John Nichols ended up in Mill Creek."

CHAPTER 6

PUNISHMENT

Ma stood by the kitchen table, her arms akimbo, glaring at Hannah.

"Well?"

"I never meant to hurt him, Ma," Hannah said. "I just wanted to teach him a lesson."

"I swear, Hannah Miller, if you don't learn to control that temper of yours you'll kill off every eligible suitor in the town of Boonville." She shook her finger. "Do you want to die an old maid?"

"No, Ma," Hannah said. Then she giggled as she puckered her lips, sucked in her cheeks and squinted . . . like she had just taken a bite of a sour pickle. "You have no idea how I suffer," she said in a high-pitched, quavering voice.

"Hannah! It's not right to poke fun at other people's misfortune. It's not your Aunt Mary's fault that her beau ran off with her best friend."

"But, Ma," Hannah said, "she's such a sour puss even Pa calls her Mary Pickles."

The hint of a smile tugged at her mother's lips. "Your pa doesn't help his sister with his constant teasing," she said.

Hannah hung her head. "I'm sorry, Ma".

"Phew. You smell like a stable."

"I know, and I'm so cold I don't think I'll ever get warm."

"Come here by the stove and take off your wet things."

Hannah handed off her smelly cloak and then slipped out of her apron. "Oh no," she said, looking down at the dark brown stain on the skirt of her everyday gingham dress.

"No sense crying over spilt milk," Ma said. She

held out her hand for the dress. "You can do your washing as soon as you get into some dry clothes.

Hannah's face fell. "But, the soap burns my hands and the scrubbing board rubs my knuckles raw."

"Maybe next time you're about to lose your temper, you'll remember that."

CHAPTER 7

BAD NEWS

"How can you stand to do the wash every week?" Hannah asked, wincing with pain as she flexed her fingers. "I can hardly bear to wash one stocking."

Ma spread thick, yellow salve over Hannah's skinned knuckles.

"I guess your hands get tough when you've done it as long as I have," she said, patting off the excess salve with a piece of clean cloth. "Better set the plates out for supper, now. Pa will be home before long."

"Hi, Pa," Hannah said, as she laid the last spoon on the table.

He waved to her from the back porch, his clothes and hair covered with a fine powder, like they were every night when he came home from the Boonville Mill. Clouds of dust billowed up as he brushed and beat at his pants with the porch broom. He came inside, coughing to clear his throat.

"How are my girls?" he said, smiling broadly.

Hannah drew a sharp breath and held it in. Would Ma tell?

"Pretty fair, I reckon," Ma said, winking at her.

Hannah let out her breath.

Pa cupped his hands, splashing cold water on his face and rubbing it dry with a towel.

"What's for supper, Martha?" he said, pecking at her cheek as he walked by. "I'm starved."

Ma carried a steaming pan of macaroni and cheese to the table.

Pa scooped a hearty helping onto his plate.

Hannah helped herself to a smaller portion, then went to the icebox for the pitcher of cold milk.

Ma sat down, her face rosy from the heat of the

stove. "Have you heard any news of the war?"

Pa set his fork down. "They say Grant's ready to move the Army of the Potomac south to engage General Lee." He stroked his chin. "This could be the beginning of the end for the Confederacy."

Hannah frowned. "Will you have to fight, again?"

Pa never talked about it much, but he had been away fighting the war for two years. He said he would never understand how he came through the bloody battle at Gettysburg without so much as a scratch, while other men were torn apart by cannon fire and Minié balls all around him. The day after that battle ended, his enlistment was up. He had walked away without a backward glance.

"I won't fight again," he said, now. "I did my part. Let somebody else finish the job, if they've a mind to." He pushed his chair back from the table. "I'll be back as soon as I feed and water Molly."

"We'll wait dessert for you," Ma said.

Hannah cleared the table, scraping the leavings

off the plates into the slop bucket under the sink. "I wonder what's keeping Pa," she said.

"Maybe he had a problem with the horse."

Hannah eyed her slice of apple pie, wishing Pa would hurry. She glanced out the window. "Here he comes," she said, brightening. Then she frowned. Pa looked upset.

"What's the matter, Pa?" Hannah said when he came in.

"Jonathon Nichols was outside hitching his horse to the buggy," Pa said. "He's going to fetch the doctor. Seems their boy took a chill today and he's running a high fever."

Hannah's heart lurched.

"How bad is he?"

"Pretty bad. They think it's lung fever."

CHAPTER 8

THE DARK BEFORE THE DAWN

Hannah tossed and turned all night. She got out of bed before dawn, padding on bare feet to the window. She propped her elbows on the sill and peered out at John's house. All she could see was a shadowy outline against the dark sky.

Hannah closed her eyes, pressing her forehead against the cool glass. Was John better? Was he worse? She wished she knew.

She stared into the darkness. There. A faint flickering light wavered where his window should be.

She hitched a sharp breath, a sob catching in her throat. He must be real sick if somebody was sitting with him.

Hannah swallowed the lump in her throat. "Please, don't let him die," she whispered.

As the sun began to rise, Hannah saw Doctor Bass' carriage by the back door. She moaned. The doctor only stayed all night when his patient was dangerously ill. Like he did last year, the night her little brother, Joe, died.

Hannah had been sent to bed that last night, but she couldn't sleep. The sound of Joe's labored, raspy breathing filled her room. She tried putting the pillow over her head, but no matter what she did she couldn't shut out the sound of his tortured breaths. And when they finally stopped, she had hugged her pillow and cried.

Hannah shook her head to drive away the awful memory. Outside, the rising sun was scattering the mists of night. She wiped her tears and rinsed her face in the bowl of water beside her bed. Then she pulled on her clothes and went downstairs.

"You're up early, Hannah," Pa said, looking up when she walked into the kitchen. He went back to rummaging through the cupboard.

"Where's Ma?"

"Next door helping John's mother. I'm glad you're up," he said, giving her a sheepish grin. "I'm not much of a hand at making breakfast."

"I'll do it," Hannah said, waving him to his chair. She grabbed a pan and took the bag of dry oats down from the cupboard shelf.

"Any news about John?" Hannah tried to concentrate on stirring the pan of oats and water on the stove.

"No," Pa said, "but your ma has sure been over there a long time."

Hannah stirred the porridge faster and faster. "I did it, Pa," she said, her words barely audible.

"What was that?" Pa moved closer, laying his hand on her shoulder.

"I pushed John into Mill Creek," Hannah said, choking back a sob. "I don't know what made me do such a thing."

Pa looked flabbergasted; then he threw back his head and laughed.

"That's not funny, Pa."

"I'm sorry," he said. "I was just thinking about the time my sister, Mary, did the same thing."

"Aunt Mary?" Hannah couldn't picture that. "What happened?"

"Well, I guess that's how she lost her beau, that and her disagreeable disposition." He chuckled. "She always was a mite feisty."

Hannah's face crumpled. "Am I feisty, too?"

"Oh, no," Pa said, patting her shoulder. "Nobody's as hard to get along with as Mary."

He took the spoon from her hand. "Now why don't you go next door and see how your friend is coming along."

CHAPTER 9

FRIENDSHIP

"Hannah!" Ma looked surprised. "I was just on my way to get you. John Henry has been asking for you."

Hannah hung her head. "He must be so mad at me," she said. "I'd give anything if I could take back what I did."

"He wants to see you," Ma said. "I'll take you up to his room."

All the curtains were pulled together to block out the sunlight. John was buried under a pile of blankets, his head propped up by two pillows. As Hannah stood back, watching Mrs. Nichols drape a wet cloth across his

forehead.

Dr. Bass rested his finger tips on his wrist.

John's eyes opened, lighting up when he saw her. "Hannah, "I'm getting better," he said, his voice hoarse.

Mrs. Nichols put her hand to her mouth and ran from the room, crying.

Hannah moved closer. His breathing was shallow, and she heard the tight congestion in the crackling wheeze when he exhaled. He coughed, a hacking, fruitless cough that shook the bed but failed to clear his airway.

"Is that true?" Hannah asked Dr. Bass, boldly. "Is John really getting better?"

"I believe he is," said Dr. Bass. "His fever broke sometime after midnight. But it will take time for him to recuperate." He tucked his stethoscope and some medicine bottles into his black satchel.

John was asleep.

"It's important for John to want to get better," Dr. Bass said. "Do you think you could come and sit with him every afternoon?"

Hannah glanced at Ma.

"I'll see to it that Hannah comes by," Ma said.

"Good. That will make all the difference in the world."

John stirred, opening his eyes.

"I'll be back to give you a dose of castor oil and apply another mustard plaster to your chest," Dr. Bass said. "That will make it easier for you to breathe tonight."

He turned to go, pausing with his hand on the doorknob. "Now don't forget, Hannah, John needs rest."

"I'll tie him down, if I have to," Hannah said.

Ma frowned, giving her a keep-quiet look, then followed the doctor out the door.

Hannah was alone with John.

Tears stung her eyes as she watched his fitful slumber. They had been friends for as long as she could remember. At least they used to be, until he started this teasing, sparring, pushing, shoving and braid pulling that made her blood boil.

"Ma says we're growing up," Hannah said, swiping at her tears. "But, why can't we still be friends?"

Then she thought about the way John's eyes had lit up when he saw her. Maybe he did still like her, after all.

Hannah reached out and lightly stroked his hand with her fingertips, then clasped it in her own. A feeling of warmth and joy filled her heart.

How long had it been since they had held hands? She couldn't remember . . . but holding his hand in hers felt so natural, like breathing or laughing.

John gently squeezed her hand.

Hannah blushed and snatched her hand away, but his eyes remained closed and his breaths even as she tiptoed out the door.

CHAPTER 10

THE WAR NEWS

Two weeks later, Hannah raced up the stairs to John's room for her daily visit.

"You wouldn't believe how warm it is outside," she said, tossing the newspaper on the chair beside his bed. "Did you eat lunch?"

John made a face. "If that's what you want to call it. Ma gives me milk toast and butter for lunch every day!"

"I hate milk toast," Hannah said, wrinkling her nose. "The bread gets all soggy and slimy soaking up the hot milk. Ma says that's so it can slide down your throat, but it makes me gag."

"It's disgusting," John said, folding his arms across his chest. "How am I supposed to get well without meat and potatoes?"

"Ma made a pot of stew for supper," Hannah said. "I could come early tomorrow and bring you some."

John grinned. "I shall dream about your ma's stew all night."

Hannah took the box of lead soldiers down from the shelf.

"Read me the war news," he said, straightening his bedclothes.

Hannah sat down and opened the latest edition of the Black River Herald. She waited for John to arrange his blue and grey soldiers in formation on his crazy quilt.

"War News – May 11th, 1864," Hannah read. "My dispatch of yesterday afternoon left the army in the midst of a terrible battle – as terrible for the time it lasted as any in the recent series of fights. In this battle, the roar of artillery was as fierce, incessant, and almost

as deafening as at Gettysburg. The battle continued till night, and darkness closed the sanguinary struggle....
Very active skirmishing all the fore part of the day merged at length into a general engagement. As the hours wore on it waxed hotter and hotter, and fiercer and sharper was the rattle of musketry, and louder was the roar of artillery."

John moved his soldiers into battle, punctuating each movement with his renditions of screaming shells and exploding shot. Soon his quilt was littered with the bodies of fallen soldiers on both sides.

"Is that all it says?" He looked up.

Hannah bent over the paper. "The fighting continued with a ferocity never before witnessed, until 9 o'clock at night, when it closed upon the bloodiest field produced in this war. The losses on both sides are stated to be very large."

John's cheeks were pink, his eyes shining. "Does it say where the battle was?"

Hannah squinted at the paper. "Somewhere around the town of Spotsylvania Courthouse, wherever that is."

"Virginia," John said, his voice rising. "Pa said Grant was moving the army there."

"You shouldn't get so worked up," Hannah said, frowning. "My pa says war is no picnic, and he should know - he was there."

"I'd like to see for myself," John said, a faraway look in his eyes. "The trouble is, by the time I'm sixteen it will probably be over."

"I hope so," said Hannah. "I've seen too many names of Boonville boys on the casualty lists."

"Aw, don't worry, Hannah," John said, grinning. "If my ma keeps feeding me milk toast and butter I won't live long enough to go to war."

CHAPTER 11

OH, IT WAS GRAND!

"Read me everything on the front page," said John a week later.

"It's just a poem," said Hannah, sourly. "You don't like poetry."

"Is it about the war?"

"Everything's about the war!"

"Please?" John grinned at her.

Hannah sighed as she unfolded the paper.

"Mustered Out
Let me lie down,
Just here in the shade of the cannon torn tree,
Here, low in the trampled grass, where I may see
The surge of the combat; and where I may hear
The glad cry of victory, cheer upon cheer,
Let me lie down.

Oh it was grand!
Like the tempest we charged, in the triumph to share;
The tempest – its fury and thunder were there;
On, on, o'er the entrenchments, over living and dead,
With the foe underfoot and our flag overhead
Oh, it was grand!

Weary and faint,
Prone on a soldier's couch, ah how can I rest
With this shot-shattered head, and saber-pierced breast?
Comrades, at roll-call, when I shall be sought,
Say I fought till I fell, and fell where I fought,
Wounded and faint."

. . . .

"That's it!" Hannah shouted, flinging the newspaper at him.

"But it's a glorious cause . . . fighting to put down the Great Rebellion, to restore the union and to destroy the evils of slavery." His eyes glowed with passionate patriotism.

Hannah shivered, goose bumps rising on her arms. "I don't want to talk about it anymore."

"If it's not over before I turn sixteen, I plan to join up," he said, stubbornly. His eyes pleaded with her to understand.

Hannah's cheeks burned, hot as fire. "You're just plain stupid, John Henry," she yelled. "I should have let you drown in Mill Creek when I had the chance."

CHAPTER 12

GROWING UP

The next day, Hannah glanced at the clock, swallowed her last bite of bread and jam, then gulped down the rest of her milk.

"Are you going to John's?" Ma asked.

Hannah looked up at her and frowned.

"Don't I go every day?"

"Rachel Nichols says you had a fight with John yesterday."

"Did she say I can't come?" Hannah's cheeks burned. "I didn't hit him or anything. It's just . . . all he ever wants to talk about is the war."

Ma chuckled. "Rachel says you tore down the

stairs and slammed the door so hard you knocked a picture clean off her parlor wall. She also said I'll have my job cut out for me if I think I can make a lady out of you."

"I'm sorry, Ma. I lost my temper because John said he was going to go to war."

What if she had gone too far this time? What if, like Aunt Mary's beau, John never wanted to see her again?

Hannah hung her head. "Does John want me to come?"

"As a matter of fact, he does," Ma said, her eyes softening. "He sent his mother over to tell me that." She took Hannah by the hand. "Please try not to have any more tantrums in John's house. You're supposed to help him get better . . . not threaten to throw him back into Mill Creek."

"Don't worry," Hannah said. "I'm sure I changed his mind about the war."

"I swear, you're getting taller every day," Ma said the

next day, around a row of straight pins between her lips.

Hannah teetered on the footstool while Ma inserted the last pin in the hem of her new dress.

"Turn around, so I can see if the hem is even."

Hannah executed a slow spin.

"Perfect," Ma said, smiling. "You're turning into a right pretty young lady."

Hannah blushed. "Do you really think so?"

"I wouldn't say so if I didn't."

Hannah jumped down and flung her arms around Ma's neck.

"Careful," Ma said, laughing and pulling the pins from her mouth.

Hannah hiked up the full skirt and pranced over to the chest of drawers. She picked up Ma's silver-backed hand mirror and stared at her reflection.

"How can you say I'm pretty?" She frowned. "I have freckles on my nose, and my nose is much too big. And just look at my skimpy eyelashes . . . and plain blue eyes. Why couldn't I have green eyes? Don't you think green eyes are nicer?"

"I think you're lovely, just the way you are."

Hannah twisted one braid around her finger. "Now that I'm fifteen, can I wear my hair down? I look like such a baby in braids."

CHAPTER 13

SCHOOL DAYS

Early the next morning Hannah strode down Main Street, on her way to the Academy for the first day of the summer quarter. Groups of students walked ahead and behind her. She preferred to walk alone.

She sniffed the early morning air, ripe with the scent of lilac and white narcissus. John loved lilacs. She wished he was there.

Hannah smoothed the skirt of her new dress and then flipped a ringlet of pale blond hair behind her shoulder. She felt for Ma's best tortoise shell combs at her temples. Thank heaven, they were still there.

She giggled, imagining the surprise in John's

eyes when he saw her with her hair down after school.

"Where's John?" Sarah Traffarn said, destroying a very pleasant daydream.

Sarah was red in the face and panting. She must have run all the way from Post Street to catch up.

"Still sick," Hannah said, walking faster.

"Hey, wait. I'll walk with you."

"Thanks." Hannah rolled her eyes.

"When are you coming back to school?" Hannah frowned at John then slammed a book on the table by his chair.

John grinned. "Hey, what did you do with your hair?"

"Never mind that," said Hannah, pulling a face. "I had to walk to school with Sarah Traffarn. And if that wasn't bad enough, she tagged along with me, all the way to your house."

John's eyes danced. "How am I supposed to pull your braids?"

She glared at him. "I thought you gave that up

after your swim in Mill Creek."

"Aw, Hannah – "

"I brought your recitation. We might as well get started," she said, handing him the book.

John leafed his way through the first few pages. "Alfred Tennyson?" He held his nose. "You know I hate poetry."

"Stop complaining and turn to page twenty-four. You have to recite this at the commencement exercise in August."

John studied the page. "This doesn't look too bad." He took a deep breath.

> "Half a league, half a league,
> Half a league onward,
> All in the valley of Death
> Rode the six hundred.
> "Forward the Light Brigade!
> Charge for the guns!" he said:
> Into the valley of Death
> Rode the six hundred."

John bowed low from the waist. "How was that?"

"Not bad, considering that's only the first stanza and this was your first attempt." She opened her book.

"I'll show you how Miss Snow said we were to recite."

She cleared her throat. "The Lady of Shalott, by Alfred Tennyson," she read, then paused, clearing her throat, again. "On either side the river lie (she waved one hand left, then right) /Long fields of barley and of rye, /That clothe the world and meet the sky; (pointing down to the floor, then up at the ceiling) /And through the field the road runs by (a sweeping motion to indicate a curvy road)/ To many-towered Camelot."

"No more," said John, covering his ears. "Show me what you did in arithmetic.

CHAPTER 14

RAINY DAYS

Sarah Traffarn was Hannah's shadow the whole first week of school, running to catch up with her every morning, then chattering like a magpie all the way there.

Hannah did her best to put up with her, but the day Sarah invited herself into John's house, offering to help him with his homework after she went home, was the last straw! She began to search for a way to sever this unwanted friendship.

Mother Nature came to Hannah's rescue the following week when the skies over Boonville opened up to drenching rains. Rumbles of thunder and flashes of jagged lightening came and went, but the rain continued, day and night.

"Thanks for driving me to school, Pa, " Hannah said on the first rainy morning.

"Do you miss walking with your friends?"

"I'd much rather go riding with you," Hannah said, smiling. "Sarah talks my ear off."

Pa chuckled. "I'll leave the horse and buggy for you at the Livery Stable on Water Street and walk to the mill from there."

Hannah slogged through the flooded streets to the Livery Stable after school, with Sarah on her heels.

"I'll drive you home first, so you won't have to walk in the rain," Hannah said, sweetly.

"I won't hear of it," Sarah said. "I don't mind walking home from John's."

Hannah's face darkened. A headache throbbed behind her eyes.

When they got to John's house, Hannah ground her teeth and cracked her knuckles, while Sarah simpered and shamelessly flirted with John.

By the time Hannah went home, she was determined to put a stop to this. If she didn't, she would probably end up drowning them both in Mill Creek

"Isn't the rain ever going to stop?" Hannah asked on the morning of the third straight day.

"I reckon it will, someday," Pa said.

She looked out at the horse from the shelter of the buggy. Rain cascaded down Molly's back and trickled off the end of her nose.

"If it doesn't quit soon," Hannah said, "poor Molly will mildew."

Pa laughed, bringing the buggy to a stop in front of the Academy.

"Do you want me to come for you at the mill after school?"

"I should be done by four," Pa said, handing down her lunch pail.

Hannah smirked as she took hold of her pail. The solution to her problem with Sarah was hidden inside.

"I'll sure be glad when John comes back to school," Hannah said, grimacing as she picked up the hefty strap of books. "Then he can carry his own homework."

"I'm sure John will be glad to carry *your* books, once he's feeling better," Pa said, pointedly.

"Pa! He'll do no such thing."

CHAPTER FIFTEEN
RATS LOVE CHEESE

Hannah looked up from her slate when she heard the clanging of the firehouse bell. The clock on the school room wall said twelve o'clock. Unrelenting rain pattered on the roof.

"Lunch time, students," said Miss Snow. "Put away your readers and slates. I'm afraid we'll have to eat at our desks again."

Hannah shoved her slate and chalk into the open space beneath her desk top, careful not to upset the bottle of ink in the ink well.

"Isn't the noon bell ringing longer than usual?" asked Sarah Traffern, through a mouthful of buttered bread, most of it glued to her protruding front teeth.

Hannah suppressed a gag, then smiled to herself as she peeled the wrappings off the hunk of limburger cheese in her lunch pail.

Sarah wrinkled her nose at the stench that wafted from Hannah's pail. She slid a few inches closer to the other end of the bench.

Hannah took a generous bite of the stinky cheese and then leaned close to Sarah's ear. "Maybe they want to be sure the men at the mill know it's time for lunch," she said, exuding limburger fumes in Sarah's face.

Sarah gagged and slid all the way to the end of the bench.

Hannah washed her mouthful of cheese down with a swig of milk, then took another bite, dabbing at the corners of her mouth with her hanky to hide a triumphant smile.

"Are you sure you don't need a ride?" Hannah asked after school.

"I'm sure," Sarah said, sidling away. "Martha

Walker asked me to ride with her."

Hannah grinned, watching Sarah and Martha splash through the puddles arm in arm, giggling like conspirators. She waited until they rounded the corner, before she ventured out into the rain.

By the time she got to John's, the rain had finally stopped. Hannah hitched the horse to the hitching post, then ran inside.

"Good afternoon, Mrs. Nichols," Hannah shouted as she loped by, taking the stairs two steps at a time. She burst into John's room.

"Where's the fire?" said John, laughing.

Hannah was pleased to see no sign of Sarah Traffarn. "I have to pick Pa up at the mill at four."

"We have plenty of time," John said. "Did you get my arithmetic lesson?"

Hannah pushed her hood back and peeled off her cloak, tossing it on the bed.

"Algebra," she said. "It's kind of complicated."

They bent over the book together.

"Phew," John said, holding his nose. "What have

you been eating . . . rotten meat?"

Hannah bristled. "If you don't like the way I smell, John Nichols, maybe I should just go home." She glared at him, then turned to go.

"Aw, Hannah, don't go." John grabbed her by the arm, baring his teeth and making rat noises. "I'm a rat . . . and you know rats love cheese," he said. He pulled her close, sniffing at her lips. "Mmmmm, limburger."

Her cheeks burned. She swayed, dizzy from the nearness of his lips, which lightly brushed hers, sending a warm sensation all the way down to her toes.

Startled, she pushed him away. "Are you out of your mind, John Nichols?"

John threw his head back and laughed. "It's after four," he said, as if nothing had happened.

"I gotta go," Hannah said, running from the room.

CHAPTER 16
WHERE IS HE?

Hannah had been sitting in front of the Boonville Mills waiting for Pa since a little after four. A few workers straggled out of the mill from time to time, but there was no sign of Pa.

Maybe he got mad because she was late and decided to walk home. Or, maybe he hitched a ride with Mr. Nichols. In any case, he was probably home right now, waiting for her and getting madder by the minute.

"Pile on the agony," said Hannah, turning the buggy toward West Street. "I might as well go home and take my medicine."

"He's not here? Where is he?"

"I don't know," Ma said, looking worried. She carried two plates of salt pork and boiled potatoes to the table. Her hands shook as she set them down.

"Shouldn't we wait for Pa?"

"He'll be along any minute. I'm keeping his plate warm on the back of the stove."

"What could be keeping Pa?" Hannah said an hour later. He had never been this late before, except for that time there was a fire in the village.

"Maybe we didn't hear the fire bell," Ma said, as if she had read Hannah's thoughts. "I'll bet he's with the Fire Company somewhere, putting out a fire."

But if there had been a fire in the village, the acrid smell of smoke would have reached West Street by now.

"The noon bell did ring a long time today," Hannah said, hoping Ma was right.

They sat a while in silence, their food untouched, the milk gravy congealing into globs of grease. The only sound was the measured ticking of the kitchen clock, which sounded louder than usual.

Ma lit the kerosene lamp at dusk and set it on the table Hannah stared into the flame. Where could he be?

Finally, Ma picked up their plates and headed for the sink. "I'm not going to sit here worrying myself sick," she said. "I'm going down to the Fire House and find somebody who knows where your father is!"

Somebody rapped on the door.

Hannah jumped.

The plates slid out of Ma's hands, clattering onto the floor and shattering into jagged shards of china.

CHAPTER 17

THE TWO SISTERS

Hannah sprang from her chair and yanked the door open.

"Mr. Nichols –"

"Evening, Hannah, is your Ma? . . .."

Hannah whirled to see what Mr. Nichols was staring at, then gaped, slack jawed.

Ma was on her hands and knees, weeping as she wiped up the spilled food with the dish rag. In her other hand she clutched broken china, blood dripping from one finger.

Mr. Nichols ran to help her up.

Hannah raced for the broom.

"I'm sorry I startled you, Martha," Mr. Nichols said. "I came to tell you about the break."

Ma dabbed at her tears with her hanky, then wrapped it around her bloody finger. "I was going out to look for Joe," she said, looking dazed. "He didn't come home for supper."

Mr. Nichols looked contrite. "I should have come sooner. But surely you heard the fire bell?"

Hannah stopped sweeping and nodded her head.

"Yes," Ma said, "but I thought it was the noon bell for the mill."

"So did we . . . at first," Mr. Nichols said. "But when it kept on ringing, we ran down to the fire house. That's when we found out there wasn't any fire – there was a break in the canal."

"Oh," said Ma and Hannah at the same time.

"Seems like all that rain caused a big slide near lock 31 in the gorge," he said. "Tons of shale and mud slid into the canal, breaching the bank and sending water and several feet of the canal down to the Lansing Kill

River at the bottom of the gorge.

Hannah shivered, picturing a boat loaded with people crashing through the canal bank and careening down to the bottom of the gorge.

"Good Lord," Ma said. "Was anybody hurt?"

"No, Ma'am. Just the profits of the boat owners who planned on traveling back to Rome tonight. They'll be lucky if they see Rome three days from now." He laughed. "They'll have plenty of time to sharpen up their card playing skills, while they wait for the work crew to repair the bank."

"Where's Pa?" Hannah asked, wondering why they both seemed to have forgotten all about him.

"Oh, he stayed to work with the repair crew," Mr. Nichols said. "He made me promise to come and tell you, so you wouldn't worry." He looked down at his shoes and coughed. "I guess I'd better get back home."

"How come Pa didn't come home with Mr. Nichols," Hannah said when he was gone.

"I'm sure he stayed for the pay," Ma said. "He

can make more money in a few days fixing a break then he makes all week at the mill." She smiled, the worry lines fading from her brow. "I don't care, as long as he's all right. As soon as the break is fixed, your pa will be back, jingling money in his pockets like a rich man."

When Pa came home three days later, he threw his arms around Ma, picking her up off her feet and swinging her around and around.

"Put me down, Joe Miller," Ma said, laughing.

Hannah watched with amazement. She had never seen Pa do anything like that before.

When he set Ma down, he waved a fistful of greenbacks in the air.

"That's a lot of money," Ma said, straightening her apron.

"It's only the beginning," Pa said. "I got a job on the canal."

"But, you already have a job . . . at the mill," Hannah said.

"Yes," Pa said, frowning, "where I'm cooped up

in the dust all day; the pay is so poor we barely get by."

Hannah reeled back, shocked. Pa had worked at the mill for as long as she could remember. The thought that he hated working there had never occurred to her.

"What will you do on the canal?"

"I have a chance to be steersman," he said, "on the Two Sisters, out of Westernville." His eyes filled with longing. "I'd be working the tiller, keeping the boat on course, traveling the Erie between Albany and Buffalo."

He shot Ma a pleading look. "Just think, Martha. I'll make a lot more money than I bring home from the mill."

Hannah frowned. She turned and stared out the window. "How long would you have to be away?"

"Not long, Hannah," he said. "Maybe a week or two at a time, and I'll be home for the whole winter once the canal freezes over."

Hannah whirled to face him. "What about us? What are we supposed to do while you're gone?"

Tears stung her eyes. Without waiting for his

answer, she ran out of the kitchen and stomped up the stairs to her room.

She flung herself across her bed. If Pa went off on the canal, she would get stuck doing all his chores. She would be the one who looked after the horse and cleaned out the stall, slopped the hog, weeded the garden and ran all the errands – to the store and the post office, and who knew where else? She wouldn't have any time to herself, and no time at all to spend with John.

Hannah pounded her fists into her pillow. Big angry tears plopped onto her quilt.

What right did Pa have to be going off on a lark on the canal, leaving her and Ma to do all the work?

CHAPTER 18

THE LOCKET

When Dr. Bass finally declared John well, Hannah looked forward to their long walks to and from school. Most days, it was the only time she got to spend with him. With Pa gone, the rest of her time was taken up by chores.

"Hi John," Sarah Traffarn said, the first morning, her voice breathy.

"Morning, Sarah," John said, giving her a lazy smile.

Hannah fumed. "John and I were talking about private matters," she said, fixing Sarah with a withering glare.

John cocked his eyebrow, grinning. "Why Hannah, you don't mean to say your recitation is a private matter?"

Hannah ground her teeth and turned her back on John, but not before she saw Sarah batting her cat-green eyes at him.

After school, while Hannah did her chores, she worried that Sarah might be at John's, knowing full well that she couldn't be.

What if Sarah was there? What if John decided he liked her better? Hannah shook her head. She was probably imagining things. After all, she never actually saw Sarah going in, or coming out of his house.

It was the middle of July before Pa came home again. He swaggered in unannounced, full of talk about the canal.

"Captain Bray . . . he says I'm the best steersman he ever had," Pa said. "And he's a man who don't give out compliments freely. He's a busy man you know. He has no patience for anyone or anything that gets in the way of a scheduled run. Why, he gets all riled up if he's just a few hours late getting his goods to market."

"He sounds like a hard man to please," Ma said, looking worried.

"Oh, he's not so bad, so long as you do your job right, although he did fire his last steersman . . . just for taking sick for a day or two." Pa frowned, rubbing his hand across the stubble on his chin. "But, I don't have to worry about that, I'm healthy as a horse."

"How long are you home for, Pa?" Hannah was looking forward to spending more time with John.

"Not long," Pa said, looking guilty. "I'll have to start back to the boat in half an hour."

"Half an hour?"

Hannah winced. She hadn't meant for her words to be so loud and sharp.

"But, Joe – " Ma looked disappointed, too.

"I know, Honey, but wait till you see the nice trinket I got for you from a fancy shop in Rome." He pulled a small, black velvet box from his shirt pocket and handed it to her.

"Oh," Ma said when she lifted the cover.

"What is it, Ma? Can I see?"

"The most beautiful gold locket I've ever seen." She held it up for Hannah to admire, then threw herself at Pa, twining her arms around his neck.

"I'll try to get home again soon," Pa said, kissing her cheek before he let go of her.

"Be a good girl, and help your ma," he said, giving Hannah a hug.

CHAPTER 19

THE LONG DRY SUMMER

After the June rains, the rest of the summer was hot and arid. By the first part of August the well behind Hannah's house was nearly dry. The garden, usually filled with plump vegetables and crisp lettuce by now, was so dry the plants were stunted and withered. Even the green tomatoes threatened to shrivel and toughen on the vine.

Now, in addition to all her other chores, Hannah had to carry pail after pail of water to the garden from the creek. Otherwise there wouldn't be any juicy tomatoes, tender sweet corn, or pumpkins for pies. And worst of all, no buttery baked winter squash.

"Did you remember to water the garden today, Hannah?" Ma asked one evening.

"Yes, Ma." Hannah leaned back in the porch swing, fanning herself with last week's Black River Herald. Her perspiration soaked bodice clung to her damp chemise, which in turn plastered itself to her sweaty skin.

The long drought had slowed the creek to a trickle and she had been forced to make several trips to get enough water for the thirsty plants.

"I'm not looking forward to going to bed tonight," Ma said, sighing. "It's too hot to sleep."

Hannah nodded, forgetting it was too dark for her mother to see.

A hot breeze drifted across the porch. Fireflies flitted over the lawn, emitting hypnotic flashes of light. Hannah yawned, logy from the heat and the sing-song-call of the crickets.

"How come you never wear the locket Pa gave you?" Hannah waved the newspaper, but it didn't seem to move the heavy air.

"I'm waiting for your pa to come home long enough to take us out to dinner." Ma chuckled. "It seems a shame to wear a fancy necklace just to peel potatoes or scrub floors."

Hannah glanced at the Nichols' front porch. It was too dark to tell if anyone was sitting there.

"You haven't seen much of John Henry lately," Ma said, like she had read Hannah's mind.

"How do you always know what I'm thinking?" Hannah said, glad the darkness hid the blush that warmed her cheeks.

"I was a lot like you when I was young," Ma said. "I've always known you didn't hate that young man quite as much as you said you did."

"He sure makes me mad, sometimes. Like that time he said he was going to sign up for the war."

"Do you think he will?"

"I don't know. He's all fired up about the cause, and I'm afraid he's just bull-headed enough to do it."

Ma slipped one arm around her shoulder. "Sometimes we ladies have to accept things we don't like in order to please the one we love."

"I can't do that," Hannah said, fighting back tears. "Not without a fight." She lifted her head from Ma's shoulder. "You're different," she said. "You don't complain no matter what Pa says or does."

Ma chuckled. "If I had my way your Pa wouldn't be cavorting off to Buffalo on a canal boat. He'd be sitting right here on this porch where he belongs." She brushed the moist tendrils of hair from Hannah's forehead, then kissed her cheek.

"Try to remember, Hannah, he's doing this for us."

CHAPTER 20

CANNING

"Hurrah," John said, jumping into the air and clicking his heels together. "No more school until December."

"Hooray," said Hannah, without feeling. When would she get to see John, now?

She walked along in gloomy silence for a few minutes, trying to think of something else to talk about.

"Ma and I have become kindred spirits since Pa left," Hannah said. "I can't tell you how many times she says exactly what I was just thinking."

"That's scary," John said, pulling a face and pretending to gag. "I wonder if that's what happens when people marry."

"What's wrong with that?" Hannah looked daggers at him.

John smirked, then burst out laughing as he dodged a swat. "Didn't you say you had to go home and help your ma with the canning?"

Hannah's face fell. "I gotta go," she said, then took off running.

Hannah opened the kitchen door, reeling back from the suffocating heat. Steam billowed from the big kettle of water that simmered over the hot fire in the cook stove.

Ma looked up from the chopping board, hands dripping with tomato juice, red as blood. She pushed a tendril of hair off her sweaty forehead with the back of one hand, smiling broadly.

"I thought you forgot we were canning this afternoon," she said, stuffing a skinless whole tomato into a Mason jar.

Hannah changed to her everyday apron and rolled up her sleeves. She selected a small tomato from the basket and pulled at the peel with a paring knife.

"Here," Ma said, taking the tomato and dunking it in a pot of hot water.

This time the peel came away from the tomato with just a touch of the knife.

"I suppose Pa is enjoying a cool breeze on the Two Sisters," Hannah said, sweat beading up on her nose and trickling down the back of her neck.

"Your pa works hard," Ma said, frowning. "He's not on a spree."

"I know." Hannah stuffed her tomato into the jar. "At least he's not off fighting on some battlefield."

Ma wiped the rim of a full jar with a clean cloth and set a lid on top. "Sometimes I think this war will never end. The Union Army has won more battles since General Grant took command, but even General Sherman's march into Atlanta failed to put an end to the rebellion."

"I wanted the war to be over before John's birthday," Hannah said, wistfully. Her lips trembled. "He turned sixteen today."

CHAPTER 21

A BIRTHDAY SURPRISE

Later, Hannah picked at her supper, the kitchen still too hot to feel like eating.

"Can I take John Henry a piece of pound cake for his birthday?"

"Sure," Ma said, cutting a generous slice and wrapping it in a clean dish towel. "You run along. I'll clean up."

Hannah looked at the sink and the worktable, both piled high with dirty dishes. Ma looked tired and kind of peaked. Hannah hesitated, torn between wanting to see John, and not wanting to leave her ma with all the work.

"I won't be long," Hannah said, deciding. "I'll finish up when I get back."

"Hannah," Mrs. Nichols said, looking down her long nose in surprise. "I was expecting John . . . he should have been back by now."

Hannah's shoulders drooped. She bit her tongue to keep from asking where John was. Ma would say it wasn't polite. "I brought John a slice of pound cake for his birthday," Hannah said. "Can I take it up to his room?"

Mrs. Nichols didn't answer; she just stood there looking frazzled. Hannah wished she hadn't come. John wasn't home, and a sharp gnawing in the pit of her stomach was getting worse. Maybe she should just go home.

"What? . . .. Oh, yes, dear, whatever you like," Mrs. Nichols said, swinging the door open.

Hannah bolted up the stairs. Suffocating heat made John's room hotter than an oven. She set the slice of cake and her handwritten card on the table beside his

bed, then turned to go. That's when she spotted the
crumpled newspaper clipping on his pillow. After a
quick glance over her shoulder, she picked up the
clipping and read it.

> Recruits wanted for the 117th Regiment,
> Lieut. II Dwight Grant and others are
> detailed to recruit for this gallant
> Regiment and a rare opportunity is thus
> afforded, of seeing and participating in a
> scientific warfare carried on by the heroic
> Gilmore, under the very walls of
> Charleston, The Babylon of Secession.

A sudden chill wrapped around her, like a cloak
of ice. Her teeth chattered and she shivered, like she was
being buffeted by a frigid January wind. At the same
time, fingers strong as iron grappled her innards,
twisting her bowels and stabbing her belly with searing
hot knives. Hannah clutched at John's bedstead to keep
from falling, doubled over by the punishing pain.

CHAPTER 22

CHOLERA

When the pain let up, Hannah headed for home. She made it as far as the outhouse before the next wave of grueling pain swept over her. It was unlike anything she had ever endured before; a powerful and consuming torment that drained her strength and filled her mind, leaving no room for any conscious thought. As long as the excruciating spasms coursed through her belly, she was helpless to do anything but cling to the outhouse seat.

With the next ebbing of pain, Hannah stumbled to the house on legs that felt as limp as overcooked spinach. She staggered in, reeling with dizziness.

"Hannah!"

She heard Ma scream her name as the pain returned. Waves of nausea rolled over her and, when she raised her hand to her mouth in a futile attempt to keep from vomiting, she felt the fiery heat of fever on her face. Retching and vomiting magnified the torture until, unable bear any more, she swooned, slipping off to a wonderful place of nothingness. Here there was no more pain, no fear. She simply floated away on a cloud of peaceful serenity, wrapped in a cocoon of soothing darkness, blissfully unaware.

From time to time, for reasons she couldn't explain, Hannah struggled to come back from her refuge, swimming up to wakefulness through a murky haze of pain and fever.

Once, she heard her mother's voice, pleading, "You have to drink." A cold metal spoon was shoved between her cracked lips. She tasted blood, then savored the cool water that bathed her dry, swollen tongue.

Another time she dreamed that John was bending near, his face close to hers. His lips moved, but she couldn't hear what he said. She tried to smile at him, before he faded away.

One day she heard someone crying. She struggled to see who. Through slits in her swollen eyelids she saw a man sitting beside her bed, sobbing. She couldn't tell who he was, because his hands covered his face.

Was she dying?

Afraid, Hannah slipped back into that timeless place between life and death.

CHAPTER 23

WHERE'S MA?

One day, Hannah opened clear eyes and looked around.

"Ma?"

The sound of her voice, weak and raspy from disuse, startled her. She was alone in a room, but it wasn't her room. Her eyes widened.

"Ma?"

An edge of panic strengthened her voice. Tears trickled down her cheeks. She lifted her head from the pillow, intending to get out of the bed, but the room spun around her at a dizzying speed. She closed her eyes and fell back on the pillow, gasping.

When the room stopped turning, she opened her eyes. The door opened.

"Hannah," Mrs. Nichols said, a warm, caring smile spreading across her face, dimpling her cheeks and crinkling her eyes.

Hannah stared. She had never seen Mrs. Nichols smile before, and she marveled at the change. Her cheeks took on a soft rosy hue and her moist eyes sparkled.

"Thank God," she said, clasping Hannah's hand. "You're going to be all right."

Looking over Mrs. Nichols's shoulder Hannah saw a shelf, and on the shelf, John's box of lead soldiers. Shock coursed through her like a bolt of lightning through a rain barrel. She ran her hand over the familiar silk and velvet pieces in the crazy quilt on John's bed.

"Why – "

"You've been very sick," Mrs. Nichols said, patting her arm. "You mustn't upset yourself or you might have a relapse." Mrs. Nichols lifted Hannah's head, fluffing the pillow.

"Where – "

"You need to rest," Mrs. Nichols said, "don't try to talk. I'll bring you some broth." She paused, her hand on the doorknob. "You must be starved; you haven't had a bite to eat for the better part of two weeks." She closed the door behind her.

Hannah stared at the door. Two weeks? How was that possible? She searched her memory, but all she could recall was an awful pain and burning fever.

She tried to get up to look for Ma, but the dizziness made her head swim. Her eyelids felt so heavy. She sighed and allowed them to close.

Sometime later, Hannah opened her eyes to find Mrs. Nichols gently shaking her by the shoulders.

"I didn't want to wake you," she said, "but you've been asleep for two hours." She lifted Hannah forward, slipping another goose down pillow behind her back.

Hannah reeled with wooziness, black spots dancing before her eyes.

"Put me down."

"You need to get used to sitting up again," she said. She sat down on a chair beside the bed, taking a bowl of broth from the tray on the bed stand.

Hannah didn't think she was hungry, but when Mrs. Nichols slid the first spoonful of warm chicken broth between her lips she opened her mouth wide for more, like a nestling seeking the next worm. She savored the rich flavor and the blessed moisture on her dry, swollen tongue. The salty broth stung the cracks in her lips, making them smart painfully, but she didn't care. Her empty stomach gurgled in delight as the broth trickled in, spoonful by lifesaving spoonful.

"That's enough," Mrs. Nichols said, too soon. "We don't want to overdo it."

Hannah closed her eyes, exhausted from swallowing a few spoonfuls of broth.

"Get some rest, now," Mrs. Nichols said, from somewhere far away.

The next time Hannah opened her eyes, Mrs. Nichols

was tying back the heavy drapes. She squinted and turned away, the glare of sunlight hurting her eyes.

"Isn't this a lovely morning?"

"Yes, Ma'am." She shielded her eyes with her hand.

"You don't look quite so peaked. Are you feeling stronger?"

"I think so," Hannah looked Mrs. Nichols in the eye. "Where's Ma –"

"Heavens, look at the time," Mrs. Nichols said, heading for the door. "I have to get breakfast for the mister."

The door closed behind her.

An unpleasant sensation of dread toyed with Hannah's mind. Her heart fluttered like a wounded butterfly, until she closed her mind to the answer she feared most. She clamped her eyes shut and willed herself to sleep.

CHAPTER 24

ANSWERS

When Mrs. Nichols came back, she plopped another down pillow behind Hannah's back and set a wicker sick tray across her legs.

"Take your time and try not to spill the tea," she said. "I'll be back later."

The steaming mug of hot tea was laced with honey. Next to the tea Hannah found a thick slice of homemade bread, toasted and lightly buttered.

This time Hannah wolfed down the food and gulped the tea, her reawakened appetite demanding to be satisfied. She ate hungrily, finishing every crumb of the toast and drinking every drop of the sweetened tea, then she fell back on her pillow, exhausted.

Hannah roused at the sound of the door opening.

"What's this?" Dr. Bass said, feigning surprise. "I thought this was John Henry's room."

"I don't know why I'm here," Hannah said, tearfully. "I don't know where my ma is, either."

Dr. Bass lifted the tray off the bed and set it on the floor.

"My dear child," he said, taking her hand. "I will answer your questions, but you must promise to be brave."

Hannah met his eyes, searching for hope.

Dr. Bass looked away, patting her hand.

The butterfly in Hannah's heart beat its wings hard against her chest, taking her breath away. She stared at the ceiling, her lips quivering.

"When you came down with cholera, your ma carried you upstairs and put you to bed. Then she ran all the way to Post Street to get me. By the time I got here you were unconscious."

He shook his head. "I was afraid we were going to lose you. Your ma cared for you day and night, she refused to leave your side. After two days, she fell ill herself."

"Oh, no," Hannah said. She looked Dr. Bass in the eye. "Is she better?"

"No," Dr. Bass said, softly. "Your ma wasn't strong enough to get better. She died three days later. There was nothing I could do."

He looked away, pulling off his spectacles and swiping a hand across his eyes, as if he couldn't bear to look at her; couldn't stand to see her pain.

Hannah's eyes burned. She should be crying, but she stared at him dry-eyed.

"Does Pa, know?"

Dr. Bass nodded. "He came home for the funeral, but he had to go right back or risk losing his job. He sat by your bed and cried like a baby, because he didn't want to go."

"I think I remember," Hannah said, feeling empty . . . as if her life had drained out of her. She shook her head, slowly.

Why was he telling her this? Ma couldn't have

died. She wasn't even sick.

"Your pa carried you here so Mrs. Nichols could look after you," Dr. Bass said.

Hannah stared at him, unseeing. Tears blurred her eyes.

Dr. Bass opened his satchel and took out a small bottle of pink liquid.

Hannah watched through her tears, as he poured out a spoonful and lifted it up to her mouth.

"This will help you rest," he said.

Hannah parted her lips, letting the bitter liquid wash over her tongue. She swallowed, then gulped the water Dr. Bass offered to rinse away the foul taste.

By the time he closed his satchel and went out, a powerful sleepiness had numbed the aching hole where her heart used to be.

Sometime during the night Hannah woke up, crying. She slid off the bed and crawled to the window, pulling herself up on her elbows on the sill. Bright, silvery moonlight made the scene outside as bright as day.

Hannah stared out the window at her house, sobbing. There, on the porch . . . that's where they sat together after supper. And there, behind the darkened kitchen window . . . Ma would never cook supper again.

Oh Ma," Hannah whispered, looking up at the stars. "How am I supposed to get along without you?"

CHAPTER 25

JOHN

After Dr. Bass told Hannah about her ma, no one said another word about her. Mrs. Nichols did look her in the eye, now. And when Dr. Bass came to call, he was brisk and professional.

Hannah curled up inside herself, playing along with their game of pretend by day, saving her tears for the long nights.

"Where's John?" Hannah said, a few days later. She stiffened, fearing the worst when Mrs. Nichols left the room without answering.

Mr. Nichols came to her room after supper.

She searched his eyes, afraid of what she might see there . . . but Mr. Nichols smiled, and he didn't turn away.

"You knew John had his mind set on signing up for the war when he turned sixteen," he said.

Hannah drew a sharp breath. Her memories came rushing back.

She had come here to see him on his birthday, but he wasn't home.... Her eyes widened. He had gone off to the war!

"I remember, now," Hannah said, tears stinging her eyes. "He left on his birthday."

"No, he only went to Rome, to sign up. He got back late that evening, all excited and wanting to tell you about it."

Mr. Nichols turned and looked out the window. "He went to see you. He said he tried to tell you he would come back as soon as he could. He was afraid you wouldn't understand."

"He was right about that," Hannah said.

CHAPTER 26

FROM BAD TO WORSE

The next morning Hannah was out of bed before breakfast, searching for her clothes. A short time later she teetered on unsteady feet in front of John's washstand, giggling at her reflection in the mirror atop the chest of drawers.

"Good Lord!" Mrs. Nichols said.

Hannah whirled, in time to see her breakfast tray slide out of Mrs. Nichols's hands and hit the floor.

She burst out laughing, not sure which was funnier . . . her own reflection dressed in John's trousers and his favorite shirt, or the side-splitting expression of feminine shock on Mrs. Nichols face.

"My stars," Mrs. Nichols said, one hand clutching at her heart. "Why didn't you tell me you felt up to getting dressed? I would have fetched some of your clothes."

"I'm sorry," Hannah said, squatting down to pick up the fragments of porcelain that once held her tea and toast.

"Let me do that," said Mrs. Nichols, pulling Hannah to her feet and leading her to a chair. "You shouldn't tire yourself."

"Have you heard from John?" Hannah said, after his mother had cleaned up the broken dishes, picked up the spoiled food and mopped up the spilled tea.

"As a matter of fact, we got a letter from him yesterday. Would you like me to read it to you?"

"Yes," Hannah said, the heat of a blush warming her cheeks. "I would dearly love that."

Mrs. Nichols sat down next to Hannah, pulling a letter from her apron pocket.

"From the trenches outside Petersburg

September 25, 1864

My dear parents,

I have only a little time to write. We are here with the 2nd Brigade, keeping Johnny Reb under siege until he surrenders. A trench is a good place to fight, but a terrible place to live. I don't know which I mind more – the constant exploding shells of artillery fire, or the lice and rats. Both are our constant companions in this forsaken place.

I am happy to hear Hannah is recovering. I long for the day I can come home, and tell her she was right – war is not at all what I expected. There is very little glory and too much misery and suffering on both sides.

Our trenches are so close to the rebels' that we can talk to them at night. They have no food most days, but we are well supplied with rations by our supply trains. I don't see how they can hold out much longer. This War is winding down and will soon be over. I have to believe that if I am to survive.

I send you my love and my undying gratitude for all you have done for Hannah. Your kindness to her can never be repaid, dear mother. I will spend the rest of my life trying to make it up to you. Please tell Hannah I will come home to her soon.

Until we meet again, I hold you all in my heart.

Your loving son,

John Henry Nichols"

Hannah's eyes brimmed with tears. "I pray he will come home soon."

Mrs. Nichols sighed, dabbing at her own tears with her hanky. "I'm very proud of him," she said, "but I'm so worried . . .." She got to her feet, stuffing the letter into her pocket.

"I'll get you some clothes," she said, heading for the door. "Your Aunt Mary is coming this afternoon. I doubt she will want to see you dressed like a boy."

CHAPTER 27

AUNT MARY'S SURPRISE

Hannah gaped at the closed door. She groaned. "Aunt Mary?"

Pa's sister, Mary, never brought sunshine with her when she came. Instead, she wore her misery draped around her shoulders like a blanket of gloom. And she never had a good word to say about anybody or anything.

Hannah parroted her aunt's perennial complaint, rolling her eyes: "Through no fault of my own, I was put here to suffer through this lonely, miserable life."

She grimaced. "The best I can hope for is a short visit," she said.

Mary Miller swept into John's room at one o'clock sharp, advancing on Hannah like a battleship bearing down on a defenseless rowboat.

She was dressed in somber black from head to toe. Even her stylish black jocket hat, which should have sported a colorful rooster feather for trim, was decorated with glossy, black feather. Hannah gaped at the feathers, picturing her aunt savagely plucking them from the tail of some unfortunate crow.

Her black, silk jacket bodice was plain and unadorned by braid, ribbon or fringe. The full expanse of her voluminous black, satin skirt was every bit as austere.

Hannah hid a smile behind her hand, wondering if her crinolines and bloomers were black, too.

"I'm glad to see you out of bed and dressed," her aunt said, briskly. "I've told Rachel Nichols to pack your things, since *she* says you're not well enough to do your own packing. She better be quick about it," she said, peering at the watch that hung from a chain around her neck. "We have to be at the feeder basin before the next boat departs for Rome."

"I don't understand –"

"I don't have time for idle chatter." Aunt Mary said, glaring at her. "There's little to be gained crying over spilt milk. Now get up and collect your things."

Tears stung Hannah's eyes. She glowered at her aunt.

"Good," Aunt Mary said, her smile frosty. "Use your anger to rise above your troubles, just as I have had to do."

Hannah gathered up her hairbrush and comb, furtively studying her aunt as she did so. Aunt Mary's complexion was pallid, her transparent skin stretched too tightly across the sharp angles of her cheeks and beak-like nose. Deep lines etched around her mouth enhanced her pinched expression.

Mrs. Nichols bustled into the room with an armful of Hannah's clothes. She dropped them onto the bed, then began to separate them into piles of bloomers, camisoles, dresses and aprons.

"Rachel!"

Aunt Mary's voice was frigid, and scathing.

Hannah stiffened, gritting her teeth.

Rachel Nichols stared at Mary Miller, her eyes wide, her lips trembling.

"Anyone with half a brain could see you have brought too much," Aunt Mary said, giving her a contemptuous look. "As usual, I shall have to do it myself!"

She sailed across the room, like a sentinel thunder cloud heralding a storm.

Hannah remained rooted to the floor while her aunt rifled through her things, sniffing in disgust and flinging most of them on the floor. She pitched the few remaining items into a traveling bag.

Hannah was mystified. Aunt Mary had always been sour and unpleasant, but she had never been this mean. And why take it out on poor Mrs. Nichols? What had she done to deserve such treatment.

Hannah stared at Mrs. Nichols . . . and then all of a sudden, she knew. Her eyes widened and her mouth dropped open. There could only be one reason.

She frowned. It wasn't easy to imagine John's mother running off with Aunt Mary's beau. It was even harder to picture her cantankerous aunt walking arm and arm with John's father.

"Don't stand there gawking," Aunt Mary said, "Get your bonnet. We have to go."

"Wait," Hannah said. She took John's box of toy soldiers down from the shelf, glancing at his mother for permission.

"Oh yes, you mustn't forget your books," Mrs. Nichols said.

"Books?" Aunt Mary whirled around, her eyes flashing. "I don't have room for another thing in this bag. You'll have to carry them yourself."

"Yes, Ma'am," Hannah said, winking at Mrs. Nichols when Aunt Mary turned her back.

Mrs. Nichols took her by the arm and helped her down the stairs.

Hannah blinked at the glare of the late September sun. She stumbled along behind Aunt Mary, glad for Mrs. Nichol's hand at her elbow to steady her faltering steps.

"You need to snap out of it and stop moping around," Aunt Mary said, flinging the words over her shoulder.

Hannah stuck her tongue out at her back.

Mrs. Nichols helped Hannah into the rented one-horse shay, and tucked a beaver robe across her knees.

Aunt Mary scowled. "I don't understand why Jonathon couldn't drive us down to the canal basin."

"He sends his apologies," Mrs. Nichols said, keeping her eyes down. "He couldn't get away from the mill."

Mary Miller snorted. "I'll just bet he couldn't!" She locked eyes with Rachel Nichols, then blinked and looked away.

"I suppose I owe you a debt of gratitude, Rachel," she said, her words dripping with self pity, "I see that Jonathon Nichols is still a spineless man."

Without warning, she slashed the horse's neck with a riding whip. The horse lurched wildly, tipping the shay up on one wheel.

Hannah screamed and clung to the seat.

"Whoa," Aunt Mary shouted, raking the startled horse's mouth with the metal bit until he stopped, his eyes rolling.

"Tell Jonathon I'm sorry I missed him," she said, her voice icy. She flicked the reins and the horse broke into a trot.

"Goodbye," Hannah called to Mrs. Nichols. She fell back against the cushioned seat, exhausted.

CHAPTER 28
BOUND FOR ROME

Hannah wrinkled her nose at the acrid odor of stale perspiration mixed with a cloying scent of flowery cologne.

She opened her eyes. She was lying on a cot in a cuddy on the canal boat. She took a deep breath of the stale air, trying to remember how she got there.

"Get up," Aunt Mary said, bending close to her face and suffusing the musty air with the overpowering scent of onions.

Hannah remembered. "Are we in Rome, yet?"

"No, not yet. We just locked through the Five Combines in the gorge. The captain's wife has made dinner."

"I'm not hungry," Hannah said, turning her back and closing her eyes.

Some time later, Hannah was awakened by the drone of a mosquito circling her ear. She sat up, scratching a fresh bite on her neck, then swatted at the mosquito.

Water slapped against the sides of the boat, but the boat wasn't moving. Outside, men called insults and curses at each other from the deck. Streaks of late afternoon sunlight filtered through the cracks in the cabin roof overhead.

"Hannah!"

She gritted her teeth, closed her eyes and made a wish. But when she opened her eyes, Aunt Mary poked her head in the doorway nonetheless.

"Get up. Samson is waiting with the carriage."

Hannah groaned, stumbling to her feet and grabbing John's box of soldiers. She staggered out of the cuddy, squinting at the bright sunlight as she followed Aunt Mary out on deck.

The Maid of Judah had been snubbed to a post alongside a busy city street lined with horse drawn wagons . . . and one elaborate carriage.

An aged Negro in a beaver stovepipe hat and white gloves, slumped forward on the driver's seat, his lips flapping as he snored.

"Samson!"

Hannah clenched her jaw. Why did that woman think everybody was hard of hearing?

"I'm right here, Miss Miller," he said, jerking to attention. He scrambled down off the landeau carriage and ran, holding onto his hat, to the end of the gangplank.

"Don't just stand there like a ninny," Aunt Mary barked. "Come here and take my traveling bag."

Hannah rolled her eyes. Wasn't that the same bag her aunt had lugged onto the boat by herself in Boonville? Why was it suddenly too heavy for her to carry?

"I'll settle up with Captain Roe," Aunt Mary said, pulling some coins from her reticule.

Hannah watched her flounce off toward the stern.

Samson bent down to pick up the bag. "Excuse me, Miss," he said, giving her a broad smile, "I got to get this here bag for the Mistress."

"My name is Hannah," she said, responding to the kindness in his eyes.

Samson beamed. "You must be the chile Miss Mary went to fetch. If you ever needs anything, you just call on Samson."

"Thank you," said Hannah, brightening. At least there was one kind soul in Rome.

"What is taking you so long?" Aunt Mary said, from behind them.

Samson cast his eyes down, picked up the bag and ambled down the gangplank.

"At this rate I'll miss my afternoon tea."

She grabbed hold of Hannah's arm, propelling her down the gangplank.

Hannah tried to look away as her aunt hurried her past the Canal Saloon, but she still heard the clink of glasses, the plunking notes of an out-of-tune piano and the raucous laughter of the men inside.

Samson had already taken his seat at the front of the landeau by the time Hannah climbed in and fell back against the upholstered seat.

She had never been in a landeau, before The carriage wasn't new, but it was remarkably well cared for. She ran her hand across the luxurious leather seat, soft and supple as new.

Aunt Mary sat down hard on the seat facing her, making the horses sidestep, flicking their ears.

Samson's back looked as rigid as a fence post. He clucked his tongue and the matched team of coal-black horses set off on a spirited trot, their silver-trimmed harness jingling.

"We always drive with the top down, unless it's raining," Aunt Mary said, as they rode up East Whitesboro Street. She waved her arm at the carriage interior. "Isn't it elegant?" Her eyes softened. "Papa used to drive us all around the city every Sunday afternoon." And then she smiled, and her eyes sparkled and her complexion blossomed like a rose, absolutely glowing

Hannah responded to this glimmer of warmth eagerly, hoping to preserve her aunt's happy mood. "Look at those lovely gowns," she said, smiling and pointing to some women who were strolling along the balcony of the Mansion Hotel.

"Ladies never gawk, nor do they point!" Aunt Mary said, fixing her with a frosty glare.

Hannah turned away, then gawked at the Doyle Hotel, just for spite.

The front of the three story hotel was on Whitesboro Street, but the long, attached block continued around the corner and down the whole length of the first block of James Street. Signs swung from brackets above the doors of the shops, putting names to a fancy restaurant, a livery, a laundry, a barber shop, an opera house and a cobbler shop. There was even a bank and a tailor shop, too.

"There are so many stores," said Hannah. "How do you know where to shop?"

"The best stores are on Dominick Street. Samson and Delilah do all my shopping there."

Samson and Delilah? Hannah stifled a giggle. She peered down Dominick Street as the landeau crossed the intersection, then glanced at her aunt.

"Don't you ever go shopping?"

"I prefer the solitude of my home. I have no reason to go out."

Hannah shivered, a chill raising gooseflesh on her arms. Was she to become a prisoner there, too?

CHAPTER 29

MY DEAR JOHN

October 7, 1864

Liberty Street

Rome, New York

My Dear John,

I hope this letter finds you. I will mail it to the address your mother gave me before I left Boonville, but I have no way of knowing if you are still there. I pray that you are, and that you are safe.

I miss you more than I can say. My life is dreadful. I know if you were here you would help me get through this. Just telling you in this letter makes me feel better.

I hope you didn't mind my bringing your lead soldiers with me to Rome. Some days, when I'm missing you, I take them down from the closet and set them out on my bed in formation, just like you used to do. One of the Union soldiers favors you, with brown hair like yours. Sometimes I talk to him, pretending you are here.

I arrived here almost a month ago, although some days I feel like I have been away from Boonville forever. I try to make the best of things, but, as you know, I sometimes have trouble doing and saying the right things – especially when I get mad.

Is it my fault Aunt Mary makes me mad every time she speaks? She is determined to make a lady out of me, or at least that's what she tells me every day. She enrolled me in Rome Academy two weeks ago, where I will get – according to her – "a young lady's quality education and preparation."

The funny thing is I like going there. Betsy Comstock is my dearest friend, and a willing ally against my aunt. My teacher, Miss Oglethorpe, is a lovely lady with a sweet smile and a kind heart. She is very sympathetic to my position, even more so since her first encounter with my aunt.

I have learned to walk gracefully and to speak softly and sweetly - can you believe it? I'm really quite refined, until Aunt Mary drives me to distraction. Perhaps she will make a lady out of me after all.

I have come to rely on the kindness and friendship of the two wonderful people my aunt calls her "hired help." Samson is her loyal servant doing anything she commands; driving her about in her fancy carriage, serving dinner, pruning flowers, grooming and shoeing the horses and cleaning the stable. His wife, Delilah, does the cooking, cleaning, ironing, shopping and any other errands her mistress demands. I try to help her whenever I can. Some of my happiest hours are spent in the kitchen with Delilah.

Aunt Mary frowns on this, and has a conniption fit whenever she catches me there.

Pa has sent word that he will be home for the winter by the middle of next month. I am counting the days. I'm sure he will take me home to Boonville. If he does, I will spend some time with your dear mother. She was so kind to me after Ma died. I will try to make it up to her.

Please write and tell me how you are getting along. I pray for your safe return every night. My mind is never far from you. Are you still fighting in Petersburg?

Take care of yourself, and don't take foolish chances. The war has to end soon, and when it does you must hurry back to me.

With deep affection,

Hannah

February 20, 1864

Liberty Street

Rome, New York

Dearest John,

Why don't you write? Aunt Mary says I am a fool to keep writing. She says you will have fallen in love with some southern belle by now. She tells me I shouldn't believe in you, because men are all alike, and that I will learn soon enough she is right. I don't believe her.

Pa says you may have been injured or, worse yet, captured by the rebel army. I pray he's wrong about that. I look for a letter from you every day.

Christmas was bittersweet. As you may recall, I was looking forward to spending the holiday in Boonville, but that was not to be. Pa had to sell our house on West Street to pay for Ma's funeral and burial, and my doctor bill. My heart is broken. My home is gone, along with my dreams of rebuilding a life there with Pa. Gone also is my hope of seeing your dear mother. I know she would tell me how you are coming along and where you are.

Pa came home in late November. I came close to a swoon when Aunt Mary smiled in his brotherly embrace. I had never seen her smile before and was truly amazed at the sight. She is a mean spirited crab who does her best to make the same of me, but I am determined to resist her.

You would be surprised at the variety of goods available in the stores here. Boats depart Rome, bound for New York City daily, and return laden with a wealth of exquisite clothing, jewelry and exotic items from all around the world.

Aunt Mary allowed Delilah to take me Christmas shopping in the landeau. Samson drove us to Dominick Street, dressed in his full livery. I wore my new black dress with leg of mutton sleeves that my aunt had her seamstress make for me. Of course no one could see my lovely dress under my black, woolen cloak, but I still felt like a queen riding by her subjects in my royal carriage.

Aunt Mary seems to have lots of money and is well known in all the stores, even though she rarely leaves home. She told me to charge all my purchases to her account. It seems that Christmas is the only time Aunt Mary allows herself to be generous.

I made Delilah wait in the carriage when we stopped at Baxter and Jones Dry Goods store on the corner of James and Dominick Streets. Mr. Baxter was kind enough to wrap the black fringed parasol I bought for Delilah and the red silk cummerbund I bought for Samson in brown paper, so they couldn't guess what I would give them on Christmas day. Afterward Delilah helped me pick out a new pocket watch for Pa at Francis Bicknell's Jewelry store. I bought Aunt Mary a large box of her favorite tea at Perry Rathbun's Grocery.

We had a subdued holiday here, as we are still mourning my dear mother's passing. Pa gave me a precious gift that I will treasure forever - my mother's locket, with a lock of her beautiful hair inside. I wear it day and night, in remembrance of her.

All I wanted for Christmas was a letter from you, but I had none. I was forced to take what pleasure I could in the smiles and cries of delight of my family and dear friends as I presented each one with my gift. If you had come home, my dearest dream would have come true.

I am coming along first rate at the Academy, but I would rather be back in the Boonville Academy with you – even if I had to share a bench with Sarah Traffarn.

I can't bear to think about spending the summer alone with my disagreeable aunt. If you can't come home before May, you will have to look for me on the Erie Canal. I am going to ask Pa to take me with him when he goes back on the Two Sisters. But if you tell me you will come, I will endure anything to be here when you arrive.

I pray this letter will find you safe and protected by the Almighty.

With undying affection,

Hannah

CHAPTER 29

APRIL 1865

"Duck!" Hannah said, pulling Betsey Comstock down beside her.

Betsey giggled, shaking her auburn curls. "Are you sure she can't see us?"

Hannah laughed. "She sits at that parlor window every afternoon," she said, "reading her latest dime novel and watching for the landeau. She won't see us, unless she puts her book down and comes to the window, and she never does that."

"Won't she get suspicious when the landeau doesn't come?"

Hannah grinned, then sprinted around the corner

to James Street. "Samson promised to drive past her window with the top up at the usual time." she said, panting. "That should satisfy her, since she never speaks to me before dinner."

Betsey pulled a face. "How do you stand to live with her?"

Hannah shrugged her shoulders. "We get by." She glanced down the street where a crowd of people was milling around a Rome Sentinel newsboy.

"What's going on?" Betsey said.

"I don't know, but it must be important." Hannah hiked up her skirts, breaking into a run.

"News, here! Get your Sentinel News, here!" the newsboy shouted.

Hannah jostled her way into the swarm of people.

"What's happening?" she said, shouting to be heard above the din of the crowd.

"It's the war," a young woman in a pink bonnet said, her eyes moist.

Hannah's heart skipped. "What about the war?"

"We won," she said. "Lee has surrendered."

Hannah stood perfectly still, no longer aware of the noise and confusion around her.

The war was over. John could come home, now, if he still wanted to.

"Did you hear?" Betsey said, tugging at Hannah's sleeve. "The war's over. My pa will be coming home." She met Hannah's eyes, her smile fading. "Haven't you heard from John yet?"

"No." Hannah turned away to hide her tears, "but I'm sure he'll be home as soon as he's mustered out – "

Fear and doubt clogged her throat, as the lines of that awful poem filled her mind with dark foreboding: .

. . . Comrades, at roll-call, when I shall be sought,

Say I fought till I fell, and fell where I fought,

Wounded and faint.

CHAPTER 31

PEACE

"Let's go home, Betsey," Hannah said, "I don't feel like buying a pastry at the confectioner's, anymore."

"Are you sure?" Betsey looked disappointed. "A glass of cold ginger beer would be so refreshing."

"Maybe tomorrow." She turned back toward home.

Betsey chattered about her father's homecoming all the way up James Street, but Hannah hardly heard a word she said. All she could think about was John. Would he come home? Or was Aunt Mary right when she said he had fallen in love with another girl by now?

She blinked back tears. If that was true, she might never see him again.

See you tomorrow," Betsey said, turning into her front walk.

"Bye." Hannah said, waving. She hurried around the corner to Liberty Street.

"I can't go home," Hannah said, when she was sure Betsey couldn't hear. "I can't bear to hear Aunt Mary's daily diatribe about the weak character of men. Not today."

She leaned back against a gas light, closing her eyes and pressing the back of her bonnet against the pole. A dull headache pounded her temples. If only she could be alone, in some quiet place where she could sort things out. She opened her eyes and looked up.

The spire of Saint Peter's church rose high above the other buildings on Liberty Street.

Of course.

What could be quieter than a church?

CHAPTER 32

FATHER BEECHAM

Aunt Mary was a devoted Baptist, attending Sunday services faithfully. Hannah refused to go.

Pa had never been much for going to church, but Ma had insisted they go with her to the Trinity Episcopal Church on Easter Sunday and Christmas. Hannah recalled the quiet, the serenity, the knowing that she was not alone and had nothing to fear. She sighed. If only she could feel that way, now.

Hannah pulled the heavy, carved wooden door open and stepped inside. The church was cool, and dimly lit by late afternoon shafts of daylight that splashed the vibrant colors of the stained glass windows across the wooden benches and kneelers.

She savored the faint scent of burnt spice in the air, as she gazed at the scenes of heavenly figures and clouds painted high above her on the vaulted ceiling.

Her shoes clacked on the polished pine floor. Candles flickered in ruby-colored glasses on a golden rack beside the altar. The altar itself was made of ornately carved marble, and draped in green and gold brocade cloth. When she reached the front of the church, she sat down. Above the altar hung a statue of Jesus, nailed to a cross.

Hannah's eyes were drawn to the crucifix. "Dear Lord," she said, tenting her hands and sliding to her knees in the pew. "If you will watch over John Nichols, and keep him safe from harm, I will never ask for another thing . . . even if he has chosen someone else."

Hot tears scalded her eyes. Great, tearing sobs shook her body. She cried until the achy feeling in her heart became bearable. Then she sighed and closed her eyes, no longer weighed down by the burden of her fears and worries. The ache between her shoulder blades eased, and the knot in the back of her neck loosened.

"What's troubling you, my child?"

Hannah's eyes flew open. A tall man in a long black cassock looked down at her, his eyes questioning.

She sniffled, dabbing her eyes with her hanky. "I'm sorry," she said. "I shouldn't be here."

"I'm Father Beecham," he said, smiling. "This is God's house, and I'm quite sure He is happy you're here. Mrs. Driscoll, my housekeeper, makes excellent tea," he said, taking her by the hand. "Would you like to tell me about your troubles over a cup of tea?"

After that, Hannah went to St. Peter's Church every Wednesday afternoon to pray, stopping at the Rectory for tea before going home.

Mrs. Driscoll served them freshly baked Irish Scones slathered with butter, or sugar cookies, still warm from the oven.

"Why did Ma have to die," Hannah said, one day. "Sometimes I wish it had been me instead." Her hand shook, sprinkling cookie crumbs on the linen table cloth.

Father Beecham's eyes clouded. He sipped his tea. "Everything that happens is part of God's plan," he said, meeting her eyes, "all part of the fabric of our lives."

Hannah sniffled, then scowled. "Don't tell me Aunt Mary is part of God's plan," she said.

"I have no doubt of that," he said, smiling. "We are all on a journey. Everyone we meet and everything that happens along the way, are threads to be woven into our life, to teach us and to help us grow."

Hannah took another cookie. "But, why do we have to lose the ones we love?"

Father Beecham patted her hand. "Tell me," he said, "do you love your mother more, or less, since she went up to heaven.

Hannah's eyes filled with tears, but she smiled. "I love her more. I never knew how much I loved her until she was gone."

"You, see?" Father Beecham said. "Without

sorrow, our joys would never be as sweet."

"I was talking to some of the boys from the Two Sisters down by the canal today," Pa said that night at supper.

Hannah swallowed a bite of roast beef, then sopped up some gravy with her roll. Her mind churned with thoughts of John. Where was he? Why didn't he write?

"Hannah," Aunt Mary said, "ladies do not mop up their gravy with their bread."

Hannah glowered at her. Pa would be leaving in a few weeks, going back on the canal until next November. She clenched her teeth. She had to find a way to go with him.

"Captain Bray says he's looking for a new cook," Pa said.

Hannah's head jerked up, her eyes widened. "I can cook, Pa," she said.

"What are you saying?" Aunt Mary looked horrified. "Joe, you can't possibly allow your daughter to work on a canal boat. I won't hear of it."

Aunt Mary spit out the words, canal boat, like

they were pieces of rotten meat. Hannah gave Pa a pleading look.

"You would have to work hard," Pa said, his brow furrowed, "long hours without complaint."

"I will, Pa. I'll work day and night if I have to."

"I can't listen to anymore of this, Aunt Mary said. She looked close to swooning as she ran from the room.

Pa smiled at Hannah. "We leave in two weeks. Best get started with your packing."

"I will miss our visits," Hannah said, when she went to St. Peter's for the last time before she went off to work on the canal.

"Come and see us when you get home," Mrs. Driscoll said, her plump face wreathed by a smile. She winked and tucked a small sack of butter cookies into Hannah's apron pocket.

"I will," Hannah said, hugging her.

"I will pray for your safe return," said Father Beecham, "and that you will have good news about that young man soon."

Hannah blushed. "I promised God I wouldn't ask for anything more than John's safe return," she said.

"God knows what is in your heart." Father Beecham smiled. "Now run along and leave everything to Him."

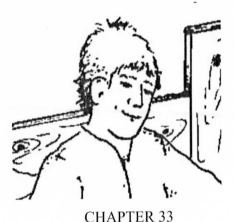

CHAPTER 33

FAREWELL

The early May breeze ruffled Hannah's hair playfully, whispering John's name as it caressed her ear.

"I'm glad I'm leaving," she said, leaning on the porch railing.

Betsey clasped Hannah's hand in hers. "How can you say that?" she said. "I'm going to miss you something awful, Hannah Miller."

"I'll only be gone until November," Hannah said, pulling her hand away. She lifted her eyes skyward, watching puffy white clouds drift across the wide expanse of blue sky. "I need to get away from here," she said, frowning. "If Aunt Mary says John is just like his father one more time, I won't be responsible for what I will do to her!"

"What does she mean by that?"

Hannah's balled her hands into fists. "She means he has run off with another girl, just like his father did when he was her beau."

"Oh . . ." Betsey stared at her, wide-eyed. "You don't –"

"No," Hannah said, shaking her head. "But where is he?" A chill raced up her backbone, she pressed her palms against her skirt. "I just want to know he's all right. I don't care about anything else."

CHAPTER 34
SIGN HERE

Pa stopped by the end of the gangplank that was drawn up to the Two Sisters. He looked Hannah in the eye.

"Are you sure you want to do this?"

"I'm sure," she said, trying to ignore the butterflies that fluttered about in her stomach. She lifted her chin, picked up her traveling bag and started up the gangplank.

"What if John comes home while you're gone?"

Hannah listened for Pa's footsteps behind her.

"He knows where to find me . . . if he wants to."

"Don't you pay any mind to what your aunt's

been saying. She don't even know John."

"I know," Hannah said, not sure that mattered.

Pa rapped on the door to the captain's quarters.

"Come in," said a brisk, humorless voice from within.

Hannah's butterflies flew helter-skelter as Pa opened the door.

"Sign here," said Captain Bray, after concisely enumerating all her duties.

He fixed her with a stern look as he blotted her signature on the contract. "You do understand you have agreed to cook for the entire run . . . from now until the canal closes in November.

"Yes, Sir," Hannah said looking up at him. She pulled her eyes away. He could break rocks with those steel-blue eyes.

"And, you are not allowed to leave the Two Sisters at any time without my permission."

Hannah nodded.

"Take her down to the cuddy and show her

where to stow her things," the captain said to Pa, like she wasn't still standing there. "There's a girl about her age traveling with us to Buffalo. She can bunk in with her."

Hannah slipped out the door and took a deep breath of the fetid air, wrinkling her nose at the mingled smells of sluggish water, decaying vegetation and manure.

"Does the canal always smell this bad?" she asked, as they made their way to the cuddy.

"For some reason it always smells worse in town," Pa said. "You'll hardly notice, once we get underway."

"Good," Hannah said, stuffing her traveling bag into the small closet.

"I better get to work. Why don't you go find that girl? Maybe she needs a friend."

Hannah laughed. "I sure do."

"Just don't forget to do your job," Pa said, frowning. "Captain Bray is an impatient man. I would hate to see you get on the wrong side of him."

"Don't worry, Pa," Hannah said, with more confidence than she felt. "Delilah taught me how to cook. The captain won't be sorry he hired me."

CHAPTER 35
JENNY MCGEE

Jenny McGee was thirteen. She had long blond hair and green eyes that crinkled when she laughed. It didn't take Hannah long to discover that she and Jenny had a lot in common.

Jenny's mother had died, too. She was traveling west with her father, where he hoped to find work. She had left the boy she hoped to marry behind, but at least she knew where he was.

"When my ma died I had to go live with my aunt in Rome," said Hannah, wrinkling up her nose. "She's so mean she hates herself."

Jenny giggled, then sobered. "I was supposed to go live

with Grandma Kelley in Albany," she said, "but Papa wanted me to stay with him, and I didn't want to leave Punkeyville." She sighed. "In the end we had to leave anyway. Papa couldn't find a job and the bank took our home."

"I'm glad you came away," Hannah said. "I think you and I are kindred spirits. You had to come, because I needed a friend."

"So do I," Jenny said.

"Let me see your teeth." Hannah, sucked in her cheeks and looked down her nose, like Aunt Mary.

Jenny laughed, then bared her teeth. "You're more contrary than Rachel Lewis," she said.

Hannah howled with laughter. From what Jenny told her, Rachel was almost as mean as Aunt Mary.

"I had to make sure you weren't Sarah Traffarn, in disguise," Hannah said.

Jenny jutted out her upper jaw, protruding her front teeth and drawing up her lip. "Perhaps I am," she said, spraying Hannah with spit.

"Hannah pulled Jenny to her feet. "You can tell

me all the news from Boonville while I peel potatoes."

That night before they went to sleep, Jenny told Hannah about her father's drinking problem.

"He hasn't had a drink since Mama died," she said, "but I'm afraid if he doesn't find work when we get to Buffalo he may start drinking again."

Hannah raised herself up on one elbow.

"What will you do if he does?"

"I don't know."

"I'll ask my pa to keep an eye on him while you're on board," said Hannah.

"Thanks." Jenny said, looking relieved. "Now, tell me your deepest secret."

Hannah fell back against the pillow and closed her eyes. She didn't want to talk about John, couldn't admit that her heart ached day and night, wondering where he was. That was too painful.

She feigned a yawn. "Now, let me see. I know. Aunt Mary's boyfriend gave her the mitten and ran off with another girl."

"Scandalous," Jenny said, arching her eyebrows.

"Tell me all about it."

"I better get some sleep," said Hannah, deciding she didn't want to talk about that either. "I have to be up before daybreak to start breakfast."

"Goodnight, then."

Hannah blew out the lantern, ignoring Jenny's disappointed look, and pulled the thin blanket up over her shoulders.

The Two Sisters slid effortlessly through the quiet waters of the canal. The boat's timbers creaked, and from somewhere up ahead, another boat's brass horn sounded.

The hypnotic thrum of muted conversation sifted into the cuddy from the deck above.

Jenny slept, her breaths soft and even.

Hannah stared into the darkness, sleepless.

CHAPTER 36

THE PARTING

The next morning at sunrise, Hannah stood bleary-eyed at the galley stove, stirring fried potatoes in one enormous frying pan, while keeping a close eye on the crackling eggs and ham in another. Heat radiated up from the cook stove, reddening her face and sending rivers of sweat down the back of her neck. Damp wisps of hair clung to her cheeks and forehead. She grimaced; the galley would be even hotter come suppertime.

"Morning, Hannah," Pa said, as he stepped into the galley."

"Breakfast is just about ready," she said, noticing the captain and the rest of the crew already seated at the cabin table. She picked up the heavy frying pan with two hands. "How's Jenny's pa?" she asked as she, scraped the browned potatoes onto a platter. "Jenny's worried about him."

"I don't see why. He was laughing and having a grand time last night, playing cards with the crew."

"Was he drinking?" Jenny would want to know.

"Drinking? On Captain Bray's boat?" Pa threw back his head and laughed. "Passenger or not . . . he'd get booted into the canal and be left to feed the carp if the captain caught him drinking."

"Jenny's worried he won't be able to find a job. She said he had a drinking problem before, when he couldn't find work."

"When we dock in Buffalo, I'll give him the name of a good rooming house," Pa said, patting her shoulder. "There are plenty of jobs in Buffalo. He's bound to find something."

"Thanks, Pa," Hannah said, dropping the wooden spoon and planting a kiss on his cheek.

Something must have gone sour between Jenny and her father the day before they got to Buffalo. Hannah didn't know what happened, but when Jenny came back from a walk with her papa before supper, she was quiet, and thoughtful, but most of all, sad.

Hannah tried to find out what was wrong, but every time she asked, Jenny changed the subject.

The next day the Two Sisters docked at the Central Wharf in Buffalo. When it was time to say goodbye, Hannah threw her arms around her new friend. "I'm sure gonna' miss you Jenny McGee," she said, sniffling.

"I'll look for the Two Sisters every day until you come back to Buffalo," Jenny said, tearfully.

"Here, let me give you a hand with those trunks." Pa hoisted the biggest trunk onto his shoulder and headed down the gangplank, followed by Jenny's pa.

Jenny brought up the rear, her shoulders drooping, her steps faltering. At the end of the gangplank she turned back to wave.

Hannah waved, staring at the bleak buildings

along the wharf, too many of them saloons. A shadow of foreboding swept over her. She wanted to run after Jenny and drag her back aboard, but she knew she couldn't do that.

"Don't worry, Hannah," Pa said, when he came back. "They'll be fine. I'll check on them next trip, if that will make you feel better."

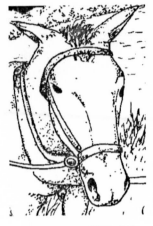

CHAPTER 37

ALBANY

After Jenny left, there was no one to help Hannah peel potatoes and shell peas; no one to help wash the greasy dishes or scour the scorched pots and pans.

She was so busy, now, that the days flew by, and she fell asleep almost before her head hit the pillow every night. In between rising and sleeping, she struggled through an endless list of kitchen chores, scrambling to get every meal prepared on time.

When the boat docked in Albany, Hannah stared at the huge piles of stacked lumber, the grimy warehouses and smoky factories.

"I thought I would be able to see the State Capitol Building," she said, frowning.

Pa patted her shoulder. "This here is the great Albany Basin, where the Erie Canal and the Hudson River come together," he said. "Someday I'm going to get a job on a boat bound for New York City." He looked wistful. "I've never navigated the Hudson."

Hannah's shoulders slumped. "What's the difference? Whether I'm on the Erie or the Hudson, I'll still have dishes to wash."

Captain Bray went ashore while the boat's cargo was unloaded, and then reloaded on a Hudson River barge bound for New York.

By the next morning, the Two Sisters' hold was full to the brim with a seemingly unending list of big city wares: tools, books, sewing threads and cloth; cooking pots, chinaware, and crates of finished clothing . . . all designed in the latest fashion.

"Here you go, Hannah," Pa said, dropping a big sack of

potatoes down on the galley floor. "The captain bought some fresh supplies at the market."

McIntyre, one of the mule drivers, slammed a barrel of flour down beside the potatoes.

The floor shook under her feet.

"Hope you're planning to make a pile of biscuits, Hannah," he said, his laugh mocking. "There's enough flour here to make a stack higher than the tallest building in New York City."

Hannah stopped scrubbing the cast iron griddle and looked around. Where was she supposed to put all this stuff?

Pa dumped an armload of fresh vegetables on her baking table, then went out for more.

Hannah swiped a soapy hand across her brow. She was already late cleaning up from breakfast.

McIntyre swung a sack of turnips off his shoulder. The heavy bag hit the floor a few inches from her foot.

Hannah jumped back, glaring at his back. How was she supposed to find the time to get more ice from the hold for the icebox, and make room for the fresh produce in the cluttered cooler? In another hour she would have to start lunch. Hot tears streaked down her cheeks and plopped into the greasy dish water.

"I should have stayed in Rome," Hannah, said, choking back a sob. "This was supposed to be fun . . . a lark, an adventure . . . canalling with Pa. I though anything would be better than spending the summer with Aunt Mary, but I was wrong . . . this is worse."

Hannah swayed, wracking sobs shaking her whole body. John was gone . . . probably for good. And this drudgery was all she had to look forward to, all she deserved.

Hannah plopped down on the sack of potatoes, the corners of her mouth pulling up in a wry smile.

She had been so sure of herself, refusing to simper and smile sweetly when John talked about going to war. But he had gone anyway, and, like Aunt Mary's beau, he was never coming back.

Hannah covered her face with her hands and cried, unable to stop until she ran out of tears.

"There's no turning back," she said, dabbing her eyes with her hanky. "I can't change what I've done, and sitting here bawling only makes things worse."

She blew her nose, sounding a lot like the captain's brass horn, then splashed cold water on her face. She took a deep breath, squared her shoulders and lifted her chin.

"I'll have this done in no time," she said, bending and yanking the door to the ice chest open.

CHAPTER 38

THE FLIGHT OF FIVES

Hannah did a lot of growing up that day. From then on she no longer crawled off her bunk to face each day with dread and self pity. She had a job to do, so she did it. She was pleased to find her chores easier to do and less time consuming.

The next evening, Hannah gazed up at the stars from her perch on the cabin roof, savoring the cool air.

"I wonder if John is looking up at the stars, too," she said, softly. "I wonder if he is thinking about me."

Hannah jumped, then let out her breath when she saw who was clambering up onto the roof.

"I'm glad you have a little time to yourself these days," Pa said, joining her on the bench.

"Me, too," Hannah said. "It feels good to have a better handle on my job."

Pa patted her hand. "I guess I'll turn in early. "We'll be locking through the Flight of Fives right after breakfast."

The sunrise the next morning was spectacular. Hannah slipped out on deck after breakfast to admire the brilliant brush strokes of red and pink that the rising sun painted above the horizon.

"Red sunrise in the morning, sailor take warning," Pa said, coming up behind her.

Hannah laughed. "I don't expect that saying applies to the Erie Canal," she said. "There's not enough water to make big waves."

Pa chuckled. "You made a fine breakfast," he said. "I should have plenty of energy to maneuver the Two Sisters through the up-locks."

Hannah watched him walk to the tiller. Pa was a

good steersman. She had never felt the slightest scrape or bump when he maneuvered the boat in or out of a lock.

The Flight of Fives at Lockport was especially tricky, though. There were two sets of five locks, one going up, and one coming down the steep rocky cliffs near Niagara Falls.

Hannah snickered. Shouldn't they be called the Flight of Ten instead?

She wandered back to the galley to start the lunch stew, humming, Buffalo Gals, while she browned the beef.

By the time Hannah had peeled and sliced the carrots, onions and potatoes, the beef was already simmering in a rich broth. She added the vegetables to the cast iron pot, tossed another piece of wood on the fire and moved the pot to the back of the stove, so it could simmer all morning.

Hannah went out on deck as the Two Sisters approached the first up-lock. She waved at Pa, who was manning the tiller, then walked to the bow of the boat.

Up ahead the mules, already unhitched from the towrope, were being led up the steep path to the top of the hill.

Two members of the crew, one on each side of the deck, used long poles to push the Two Sisters into the first up-lock. Hannah watched, proud that Pa was the reason the boat slipped straight into the lock without incident. Lock tenders in Bowler hats swung the balance beams, closing the rear gate behind the boat.

"Open the sluice," Captain Bray shouted.

Water poured in through a small opening at the side of the front gate. As the level of the water in the lock rose, so did the Two Sisters, until the boat was even with the water level in the second lock.

"Open the front gates," the captain shouted, and the boat was guided into the second lock.

The same routine was followed to lift the boat up to the third, and then the fourth up-lock.

Hannah wandered back to the stern, where Pa was busy lining the boat up with the last lock.

"What time do you think we'll make Buffalo?"

He pulled his pocket watch out and glanced at it. "If we don't have any trouble, I expect we'll dock at the Central Wharf by eight o'clock."

The words were barely out of his mouth when a loud scraping noise filled Hannah's ears, followed by a jolting shudder that knocked her off her feet.

"Ow," she said, landing hard on the deck.

"Miller," Captain Bray hollered, "What the Sam Hill are you doing back there . . . sleeping?"

Pa, who had fallen to one knee, scrambled to his feet and pulled Hannah upright.

"I'm all right, Pa," Hannah said, brushing off her skirts.

Pa raced aft.

Hannah ran after him.

"Give me that pole," Pa shouted to one of the crew. He grabbed the pole and ran to the port side.

Hannah peered over the side. She gasped, putting her hand over her mouth. The bow of the Two Sisters had swung to the left and wedged against the side of the lock.

"Be careful, Pa," Hannah shouted.

He seemed to be moving in slow motion, as if she was watching him from a great distance. The captain and crew mouthed words and waved their arms, but she couldn't hear what they said.

Pa leaned out over the side of the boat and pushed the flat of one hand against the side of the lock. The veins in his neck stood out as he pushed, harder and harder.

Suddenly, the boat broke free, jolting off the wall and pitching Pa over the side. He grabbed the rail with one hand as he fell.

Hannah gripped the rail with white-knuckled hands, staring down at him. She leaned over the side, reaching for his other hand.

"No," Pa said, panting. "Keep back. I don't want you to get hurt. I can get up by myself."

The sound of running feet raised Hannah hopes. Any minute the rest of the crew would be there to help.

Pa gritted his teeth and screwed up his face,

pulling so hard with his one arm the muscles bulged out like strands of thick rope. Beads of sweat stood out on his brow. Somehow he managed to get both hands on the rail. He drew a ragged breath, then lifted himself higher, raising his shoulders above the rail.

"Swing your foot over the side," Captain Bray shouted, running toward them. "McIntyre, haul him back on deck."

McIntyre sprinted toward Pa.

Then, without warning, the Two Sisters swung back pinning him against the lock wall.

"Pa," Hannah screamed, as his face contorted with pain.

CHAPTER 39

CAPTAIN BRAY

"You can't be serious," Hannah said, bluntly. She glared at the captain. "My father is a good worker."

Captain Bray stared at something above her head, tapping his fingers on his desk. "Your father," he said, slowly and deliberately, "has a broken leg. He can't perform his duties with a broken leg. Therefore, he must leave the Two Sisters."

"Why? Why can't he be carried down to my cuddy? I can look after him."

Captain Bray looked her in the eye, smirking, like she was too stupid to understand. "And who will perform your duties?"

Hannah reeled back, as if his sarcasm had slapped her in the face. The man was heartless, but he did have a point. There was no way she could do her job and take care of Pa at the same time.

"Very well," she said, pulling her eyes away. "I shall have to give my notice. If my pa can't stay on the boat, I will find a place for us to board until he's well enough to go home."

Hannah turned to go.

"I'm afraid you can't do that," Captain Bray said, his voice icy.

Hannah whirled to face him.

"You signed a contract to cook for my crew until the canal closes," said the captain. "If you don't honor that contract, I can have you arrested and put in jail."

Hannah stared into his steely eyes. He meant every word. Her shoulders slumped.

"I'll need some time," she said, tight-lipped, "and I'll need help to move my pa to a boarding house near the canal."

Hannah left her pa lying on a makeshift stretcher

on deck while she went to get his money from his duffel bag. She ran to the crew's sleeping quarters, found his duffel bag and plunged her hand all the way to the bottom. Her knuckles scraped against the rough canvas seam at the bottom of the bag.

Pa's money was gone!

Hannah sprinted back to Captain Bray. "Someone stole my pa's money," she said. "You have to give me some of my wages so I can pay for his care."

"No one steals anything on my ship," the captain said, scowling. "More likely your father gambled his money away."

Hannah opened her mouth to argue, but Captain Bray silenced her protest with his raised hand.

"We depart in one hour," the captain said. "The repairs necessitated by your father's carelessness should be completed by then. As to your wages, your contract clearly states that you will be paid when your commitment is fulfilled."

He sat down at his desk and picked up his pen, dismissing her.

CHAPTER 40
REQUEST DENIED

Exactly one hour after she left the boat with Pa, Hannah hurried back up the gangplank and ran to the galley to check on the stew. She expected to find the fire burned out, the stew cold and uncooked. But some good-hearted person had stoked the fire while she was gone.

Tears stung her eyes as she touched the hollow at the base of her throat. Ma's locket was gone . . . sold at a pawn shop for enough money to pay one month's room and board at the Shady Rest Boarding House. The landlady agreed to look after Pa until the money ran out.

Pa's right leg had been broken below his knee. The doctor gave him a sip of whiskey to dull the pain, then yanked on his leg to align the broken ends, while Hannah held him back by the shoulders.

She clamped her eyes shut, trying to block out the memory of his screams. He looked so sad and miserable when she left him there. And who knew how long it would be before the captain gave her permission to see him again. She sighed. Pa had better mend fast, because she had no more money, and nothing else to pawn.

That night, Hannah tossed and turned on her cot. What would she do if Pa wasn't well enough to come back to the boat in a month? Where would she get the money to pay for his room and board for another month, or more?

"I need to talk to Jenny," Hannah said, "as soon as we dock in Buffalo. Maybe she and her papa can rent a buggy and bring Pa to stay with them, until his leg mends. I could repay them when I collect my wages."

The next morning, Hannah went straight to the

captain's office. "I need to leave the boat in Buffalo," she said, "long enough to arrange for my father's care."

He peered at her over his reading glasses. "Request denied," he said, returning his attention to the papers scattered around his desk.

"Please," Hannah said, clenching her jaw. "I only need an hour or so."

"I gave you an hour yesterday. What more can you possibly need to do?"

"I have a friend in Buffalo – "

"And you think I should allow you to waste my time with your friend?" His eyes bored into hers.

"No," Hannah said, sharply.

His face reddened. He got up and opened the door. "Good," he said, "I'm glad we agree on that."

"But – "

Nevertheless he pushed her out, slamming the door behind her.

CHAPTER 41

SENECA JOE

Hannah pounded her fists on her pillow, then kicked the leg of her cot.

"You're a hateful old man," she said to the empty cuddy. "One lousy hour . . . that's all I need." She shook her head. "Now what am I supposed to do?"

Hannah sniffled, lifted her chin and swiped at her tear-streaked cheeks with the back of her hand.

She could write a letter.

Why didn't she think of that before? Every boat carried a mail bag, and letters were exchanged at every stop along the canal.

She got up and rifled through Pa's duffle bag, pulling out his pen, a bottle of ink and a scrap of paper.

The next morning Hannah handed the finished letter to Captain Bray. He stuffed it in his jacket pocket and walked away.

"Wait," Hannah said, running after him.

The captain turned on his heel. "What is it?"

"You didn't give me a chance to explain," she said, panting. "I need you to give my letter to the captain of the next boat headed for Rome."

"I will leave that to the driver," he said. "Surely you don't expect me to personally deliver your mail?"

She ground her teeth. "Of course not," she said, retreating to the galley.

The aroma of sizzling ham steak and her growling stomach reminded Hannah that she hadn't eaten supper last night. She stuffed a slab of ham in her mouth as she piled the platter high with ham and fried potatoes.

Seneca Joe, who had been promoted to Steersman as a result of Pa's injury, smiled at her when she set the heavy platter on the table. Hannah wasn't sure what to make of that. As long as Pa was on board, none of the crew had so much as looked her way.

"I kept the fire going for you, while you was with your pa," Seneca said quietly.

Hannah's cheeks burned. "Thank you," she said, then fled to the galley to fetch the coffee.

"Hey, Hannah," McIntyre called, "how come your pa left all his money behind?" He threw back his head and laughed.

Hannah clenched her jaw. McIntyre took Pa's money. She knew it, now, as well as she knew her own name. But she had no proof, and the captain wouldn't believe her even if she did.

She kept her eyes focused on the table as she served the rest of the meal. The men laughed and joked amongst themselves like they always did, until the captain took his chair at the head of the table.

"Eat hearty, lads," the captain said. "We'll reach the Flight of Five before noon, and there will be no lunch for you until the Two Sisters is clear of them."

Hannah smiled to herself. The driver was sure to find a boat headed for Rome at Lockport.

CHAPTER 42

DONNYBROOK

The Two Sisters locked through the down-locks at Lockport without incident.

When the crew gathered for lunch, Seneca Joe looked pleased with himself. His boat-mates toasted him with mugs of ginger beer.

"Where did you learn to navigate a boat like that?" asked Sal, another driver.

"Maybe he paddled his canoe over the falls at Niagara," said McIntyre. He snickered.

Seneca Joe's ruddy complexion darkened.

The rest of the men erupted in raucous laughter.

Hannah watched from the galley, wishing Captain Bray was there to settle them down.

The air in the cabin was electric with tension, the mood of the crew swiftly changing from congenial to confrontational. Unless somebody or something deflected the anger she saw building in Seneca Joe's eyes, there was going to be a fight. A donnybrook . . . like the brawls McIntyre liked to brag about.

Hannah pictured the broken chairs, the blood smeared floor, and the shards of china scattered about the cabin in the aftermath of such a fight.

"Not at my table," said Hannah, taking hold of the handle of the heaviest cast iron frying pan. She marched into the cabin holding the heavy pan up over her head like a club.

The men's heads snapped up. They stared at her, their mouths dropping open, their eyes bugging out. The hint of a smile flickered in Seneca Joe's eyes.

"Not another word," Hannah said, her words clipped, her jaw set. "You are here to eat . . . so get eating, and get back to work."

"Better do what the lady says," Captain Bray said, nodding his approval as he swept by and took his

seat at the head of the table. He picked up his tin cup, sipped his ginger beer and burped, loudly.

The crew turned their attention to their plates.

Hannah stumbled back to the galley on shaky knees.

CHAPTER 43

A NEW FRIEND

Hannah dropped the frying pan on the baking table, closed her eyes and took a deep breath. Then she hoisted the platter of fried potatoes and onions onto her shoulder and headed back to the cabin.

After that, Hannah was treated with civility and grudging respect by the crew of the Two Sisters. If any one of them made an insulting, vulgar or otherwise provocative remark, it was immediately met by loud clearing of throats and eyes rolling in the direction of the galley.

"Thanks for stepping in yesterday," Seneca Joe said the next evening. "If you hadn't, I would have been kicked off the boat for fighting."

Hannah looked up at the stars from her perch on the cabin roof. "Captain Bray is a hard man," she said, scowling "If I hadn't stopped the fight he would have fired me, too, and confiscated my wages to pay for the damages."

Seneca Joe laughed. "I think the captain was surprised you had the gumption to take on the whole crew like that."

Hannah lifted her chin. "I have to look out for myself, now that my pa is laid up."

"You let me know if there's anything I can do to help. I have a sister at home about your age."

Hannah looked him in the eye and saw he meant what he said.

"I wrote a letter to my aunt in Rome," she said, "Do you know if it was handed off to a boat bound for Rome?"

He looked embarrassed. "McIntyre got hold of your letter," he said. "He read it to the crew last night, then tore it up."

Hannah's eyes filled with tears. "I should have known better than to trust Captain Bray."

"I'm awful sorry."

"I need your help," she whispered.

CHAPTER 44

THE HOGGEE

"Are you sure you still want to do this?" Seneca Joe looked worried.

"No," Hannah said, "but I don't know any other way to get off the boat." She grabbed the bundle of clothes he held out to her and scurried into the cabin.

A light flickered through a crack in the door of the captain's office. She tiptoed past the door, then darted into the cuddy.

It was almost ten o'clock; the time the towteam was due to be switched. Sal would be tired by now, and anxious to turn in. With any luck he would think she was his relief, McIntyre.

Hannah slipped out of her clothes, except for her chemise and bloomers. She pulled McIntyre's dirty blue jeans on, wrinkling her nose at the stench. They smelled worse than a stable full of mules. She tucked her chemise inside the pants, then slipped her arms into his wrinkled, woolen shirt.

She jumped at the sound of a light knock, then opened the door a crack.

"Hurry," Seneca said, whispering, "and don't forget to smear your face with lampblack."

Hannah laced up the heavy brogans, then grabbed the soft leather hat. She stuffed her hair into the crown, then pulled the hat on. She ran her fingers around inside the lamp chimney, then spread the black oily stuff all over her face. When she finished, she took a deep breath and opened the door.

"Good," Seneca Joe said, whispering. "Keep the hat pulled down low and no matter what Sal says, don't say a word."

Hannah bobbed her head.

They crept past the captain's door, then slipped

out on deck.

The night was dark and shadowy. Thick grey-flannel clouds concealed the moon and stars.

Hannah followed Seneca Joe down to the stable, where he showed her how to rig the mules.

"Keep the flame low until Sal is gone," he said, handing her a lantern. "The mules know the way, but you'll need the light to see the towpath."

"How many miles to Rome?"

"No more than five and it's an easy stretch."

"What if McIntyre wakes up before we get there?"

"Not a chance," Seneca said, chuckling. "I slipped him some of the captain's best whiskey before he turned in. He'll be snoring all night."

"I hope you don't get in trouble for doing this." she said.

"I've got it all figured out," Seneca said. "All I have to do is roust McIntyre out of his bunk when we're pulling into Rome. He won't dare tell, because if he goes to the captain with whiskey on his breath he's all done. And, if he's not at his post by the time the captain gets up, he's done. I'll wager he'll find a way to sneak off the boat and catch up with the mules before that happens."

"I don't know how to thank you," Hannah said, clasping his hand.

"You better get going before Sal comes looking for you. And don't forget," he said, leading the first mule to the off ramp, "as soon as you give your aunt the news about your pa, get back to the boat. The captain gets real ugly without his breakfast."

The mules heaved themselves up the ramp, then down to the towpath.

Hannah paused to wave goodbye, then followed the mules into the inky darkness.

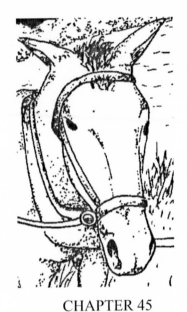

CHAPTER 45

FIVE MORE MILES ON THE ERIE CANAL

"I thought you was never coming," Sal said, scowling.

Hannah kept her head down while Sal unhitched his team and turned them around.

"Better get the boat underway as soon as I'm aboard," Sal said, starting back down the towpath.

Hannah spotted the towrope by the edge of the canal, bent to retrieve it and fasten the mule rig to the rope. She looped the reins around her waist and held them with one hand, like Seneca had told her to do. In her other hand she held the lantern.

How was she supposed to know when to start the mules? If he had told her, Hannah couldn't remember. She had never watched the changing of the mules at night. During the day the retiring Hoggee waved from the deck, but that wouldn't help at night.

Hannah stared into the darkness behind her, but couldn't see a thing. An owl hooted from a nearby tree branch, and from another direction came the hair-raising howl of a four legged predator. The mules pricked up their ears, sidestepping nervously, straining against the lines. She shivered, goose-flesh rising on her arms. Stars twinkled above her as the clouds thinned and broke up.

A bell tolled from the direction of the boat: Dong . . . dong . . . dong. Hannah let out her breath. That must be the signal.

She flicked the reins and clicked her tongue. The mules plodded forward. She held them back until she felt the towrope grow taunt, then let them to pick up speed gradually, giving them their heads when they got

up to stride.

McIntyre's too-big boots were difficult to walk in and no matter how she wriggled her toes, the rough leather chafed against her heels and the sides of her feet.

After the first hour, she hobbled along on blistered feet. By the end of the second hour, the blisters were broken and weeping, the brogans grating against raw and bloody feet.

Hannah longed to stop, so she could tear strips of cloth from her chemise and bandage her bloody feet. But that would mean halting the mules, which in turn would stop the boat. And if she did that, somebody would come running up the towpath to find out why the boat wasn't moving.

Captain Bray would fire her, she had no doubt of that, and considering his penchant for meanness, he wouldn't put her off the boat in Rome. He would wait until they got to Utica where the sheriff would take her straight to the county jail.

Hannah gritted her teeth, moaning softly as she limped on. After a while she couldn't feel her feet anymore.

When the first streaks of pale light appeared in the eastern sky, Hannah rehearsed her plan. As soon as the mules reached the basin in Rome, she was supposed to drop the lines and run. The mules would keep going until they reached the snubbing posts at the basin. After that, it would take a little more time for the boat to come to a stop. Then the crew would have to maneuver the boat to the side of the canal before anybody could go ashore.

By that time, Hannah had planned to be in Aunt Mary's house on Liberty Street.

But how could she run on blistered feet?

CHAPTER 46

THE GETAWAY

Sunrise found Hannah still limping along the towpath behind the mules. She was coming into the city limits, now, getting closer to the canal basin.

Early morning birds called to one another from the trees beside the towpath; the morning sun shimmered on the water. But Hannah was in such misery it was impossible for her to take any notice. The numbness had left her blistered feet, and hot waves of throbbing pain dogged every step she took.

Hannah willed her feet to keep moving. She studied the buildings and streets in the outskirts of the city, hoping to hitch a ride on the back of a wagon, or *borrow* an unattended horse and buggy. But there were no horses or wagons in sight.

She rounded the curve that Seneca Joe had said would keep her out of sight from the boat for a few minutes. A wooden sign welcomed her to Rome. She scanned the grimy buildings that lined the canal, grinning when she spied a saddled horse tethered to a tree between two buildings.

There was no one to be seen. The horse cropped lazily at the grass, switching his tail at the early morning flies.

Hannah hitched a breath. She had never ridden a horse before, wasn't even sure she could. But as far as she could see there were no buggies waiting to be *borrowed*. And, in a few more minutes she would be visible from the boat again. And since there was no way she could run, or even walk to Liberty Street, she had no choice.

Hannah dropped the lines on the towpath and hobbled toward the unsuspecting horse. When she got close the horse picked up his head and nickered, but he didn't run away.

"Easy," she said, grabbing his halter and stroking his neck.

Maybe it was the smell of mules on her hands, or McIntyre's scent on her clothing; whatever the reason, the horse tossed his head and sidestepped closer to her.

Hannah freed the reins and pulled herself into the saddle, biting her lip to keep from crying out from the pain when she put all her weight on the foot in the stirrup. The horse didn't move.

She looked back at the canal. The bow of the Two Sisters came around the bend.

"Giddy up," she said, kicking the sides of the horse and slapping his rump with the flat of her hand.

The horse bolted, nearly unseating her. She clung to the pommel with one hand, the reins with the other.

CHAPTER 47

YOU BETTER GIT

The horse galloped off in the general direction of Aunt Mary's house. By the time they got to Liberty Street, he had slowed to a walk. Hannah tugged on the reins, turning him into her aunt's driveway.

For the first time in her life she looked forward to seeing her aunt. To Hannah, Aunt Mary had become an oasis of hope in a desert filled with cruel impossibilities. She might fuss and scold, but she would never turn her back on her brother. She would find a way to bring Pa home.

Hannah sighed. She couldn't wait to pour out all her troubles on Delilah's shoulder.

Hannah patted the horse on the neck, tied the reins to the pommel and swung down from the saddle. She grimaced, biting her lip when her blistered feet touched the ground. She slapped the horse on his rear and then watched him canter down the street toward the canal.

She lurched onto the porch and rapped on the door.

No answer.

That was odd.

Hannah pressed her ear to the door, straining to hear Sampson's footsteps in the hall. All she could hear was the drumming of her own heart.

This time she pounded the door with her fists.

Still no one came to the door, and she saw that all the windows were shuttered.

Where was everybody?

Hot tears coursed down her cheeks, smearing the lampblack and running into grey rivers that dripped off her chin and splotched on the front of McIntyre's shirt

Hannah slumped against the door, not knowing

what else to do.

Suddenly an upstairs window was thrown open.

Hannah staggered off the porch and looked up.

"Go away," Delilah said, her eyes round, her lips trembling.

"Delilah, it's me . . . Hannah. Come down and let me in."

"You better git, before I call the police," Delilah, said, scowling.

CHAPTER 48

IT'S REALLY ME

"Look," Hannah said, pulling off the felt hat and shaking her hair loose. "It's really me."

Delilah came down and opened the door a crack. She peered through the opening, her face lighting with recognition.

"Praise the Lord!" she said, swinging the door open and pulling Hannah into her arms.

Hannah sagged against her. "I'm so glad to see you, Delilah" she said between choking sobs.

Delilah stepped back, holding Hannah by the shoulders. "What on earth have you got on, girl," she said, frowning. "You need a bath."

"There's no time for that. I have to talk to Aunt Mary, right away."

"Oh, you got plenty of time for a bath, chile," Delilah said, helping Hannah into the kitchen. "Your aunt's not here. She went off with Samson in the Landeau yesterday."

Hannah's eyes widened. "Where did they go? When do you expect them back?" She wrung her hands, her mouth puckering. "What am I going to do?"

"I don't know," said Delilah. "I don't know where they went. All I know is that Miss Miller got a telegram yesterday. She didn't tell me what it said, but it must have been bad news. She took to her bed for an hour after she read it. Then she made me pack a bag for her, quick as scat. Samson got the horse and landeau ready and they drove off. I don't think he knew where they were going, or if he did he didn't have time to tell me." She shook her head. "I don't know when they is coming back."

Hannah's shoulders slumped. "I can't stay here," she said, sobbing. "You'll have to tell Aunt Mary that Pa needs help."

Delilah's eyes got big. "What's wrong with your pa?"

"He got hurt," Hannah said, wringing her hands, "real bad. The captain put him off the boat, but he wouldn't let me stay with him." She hiccoughed a sob. "I had to leave him there, all alone."

"There, there," Delilah said, slipping one arm around Hannah's shoulder. "It sounds to me like you done all you could for your pa. You'll feel better after I get you cleaned up."

Hannah pulled away. "No. I have to get back to the boat. If you won't help me, Father Beecham will." She turned to go, but the room began to spin like a top. She wobbled, the light fading as she fell.

CHAPTER 49

THE LETTER

When Hannah revived, she was lying on Aunt Mary's bed. Delilah had stripped off McIntyre's smelly clothes and was tenderly bathing her with cool, rose scented water.

She struggled to sit up, but Delilah pushed her down.

"You're not going anywhere," she said. "When I'm done, I'm going to fetch the doctor. Those feet look like raw meat."

Hannah closed her eyes, giving herself up to Delilah's gentle care. What else could she do?

Her mind was riddled with questions. Would

Captain Bray send the sheriff after her? Would he have her thrown in jail? She shuddered.

By the time Delilah went to fetch the doctor, every inch of Hannah had been scrubbed clean, and her feet wrapped in linen towels. Two goose-down pillows cushioned her head.

She smoothed the lace at the neck of Aunt Mary's white lace-trimmed night dress. "I have never felt so alone," she said. "Pa's stuck in Lockport, Aunt Mary and Samson have gone who-knows-where, and John? . . .." Scalding tears of self pity coursed down her face. Sobs tore at her throat.

When Hannah finally regained her composure, she looked around for a handkerchief to dry her eyes. She slipped off the bed and limped to the dresser. She tugged at the center drawer, but it wouldn't budge.

She pulled harder, but the drawer was jammed. What on earth did Aunt Mary keep in there? Nobody could have that many hankies.

Hannah braced her feet and gritted her teeth, then yanked on the drawer pull with all her might.

When the drawer let loose, she gasped. The drawer was chockfull of letters, neat stacks of them.

Hannah knew she should close the drawer, knew it was wrong to read someone else's mail . . . but her curiosity was too great. She ran a finger across one stack. Maybe they were Aunt Mary's old love letters from Jonathon Nichols.

She pulled one letter from the bottom of the pile, hoping her aunt wouldn't notice if she left the top letters undisturbed.

Hannah forced the bulging drawer shut, then took a closer look. She arched her brows. The letter had never been opened. Curious, she turned the letter over, then drew a sharp breath.

CHAPTER 50

THE SECRET

The letter was addressed to Miss Hannah Miller, her name written in John's bold script.

Hannah's hands shook so badly that she had trouble opening the envelope. Her mind raced. Were all these letters from John? Why were they stuffed in a drawer in Aunt Mary's dresser?

Her eyes widened, darting over the words:

From the trenches at Petersburg

October 1864

My Dearest Hannah,

Your wonderful letter was gratefully received. I was so happy to hear that you are recovering from your illness. I was very worried about you and hated to leave your side while you were so sick, but a soldier must go when duty calls.

I wish I could be there with you. I would take care of you, as you cared for me when I was ill. But, for a while longer I am needed here, on the field of battle.

General Grant is a great leader. He is lengthening our Union lines more every day. Soon, Lee will be hard pressed to defend against such a long front, and the war will have to end. At this rate, I should be home by early spring.

I look forward to the day when I can hold you in my arms. Until then, I will hold you in my heart.

Write as often as you can. I can endure the winter's cold and all the privations of a lonely soldier's life, as long as I know you are there, waiting for me.

Goodnight my love,

John

Hannah stumbled back to bed, falling back on the pillows and closing her eyes. All those months, wondering why John didn't write, worrying that he was injured, or dead, afraid he had found someone else.

Hannah fumed. And all that time . . . Aunt Mary knew; knew he was writing, because she was stealing his letters and hiding them in her drawer.

Hannah's eyes snapped open at the sound of the front door latch. She stuffed the letter under her pillow.

Delilah lumbered up the stairs. "The doctor will come at two o'clock," she said, panting and fanning her face with her hand. She peered at Hannah.

"Are you all right?"

Before Hannah could answer, the front door opened again.

Delilah spun on her heel and ran out to the hall.

"Delilah?"

Aunt Mary? Hannah stiffened, clenching her jaw. Raw anger surged through her like a raging river.

"Miss Miller, Hannah's here," Delilah said

CHAPTER 51

WAR OF WORDS

"No," Hannah said through gritted teeth.

But Delilah was on the landing, and Aunt Mary half way up the stairs.

"Hannah," Aunt Mary said with obvious delight as she swept into the room. Her cheeks were flushed pink, and a smile illuminated her usually dour expression. "My dear child. I'm so happy to see you."

"Get out," Hannah said, giving her a scathing look. "I never want to see you again." She turned to Delilah. "Help me get dressed so I can get out of here"

"Oh, no," Aunt Mary said, fluttering her hands over her heart. "You can't mean it. You must stay . . .

I won't hear of anything else."

"How dare you?" Hannah said, tears spilling down her cheeks. "How dare you steal John's letters from me? You lied . . . telling me he didn't care and that's why he didn't write. I hate you. I never want to see you again." She buried her face in her hands.

"Oh, Hannah, I'm so sorry."

Hannah peeked through her fingers.

Aunt Mary's mouth puckered. "That was a mean and spiteful thing for me to do, but I was only trying to protect you . . . trying to save you from a miserable life like mine."

Fat tears rolled down her powdered cheeks and splattered on the bodice of her black, watered-silk dress.

Hannah dropped her hands. "I've never seen you cry, before. Not even after Ma died."

"Please forgive me," Aunt Mary said, gathering her into her arms. "I've been a bitter old maid far too long." She stepped back, smiling through her tears. "I was wrong. John Nichols is a wonderful boy."

"But, how –"

"He came here looking for you shortly after you left," Aunt Mary said, perching on the edge of the overstuffed wing-backed chair. She grasped Hannah's hands, like they were bosom friends.

"When he discovered you were gone he set off the very next day to search for you along the canal." Her eyes softened. "I knew then," she said, "how much he cared for you, and how wrong I had been to come between you." Her eyes begged for forgiveness.

Beyond the pain and remorse in her aunt's eyes, Hannah glimpsed, for the first time, the festering wound of unrequited love buried deep within.

"I understand." she said, softly, pity for her aunt overshadowing her anger. She held out her arms and drew Aunt Mary close. Hannah kissed her cheek, then fell back against the pillow

All of a sudden she bolted upright. "I forgot to tell you . . . Pa got hurt."

Aunt Mary smiled. "Your pa is going to be all right," she said. "Samson is putting him to bed in his room at this very moment."

Hannah stared at her. "But how did you know?"

"John almost caught up with you in Lockport. When one of the lock tenders told him about your pa, he went directly to the boarding house, then telegraphed me. He stayed with your pa until Samson and I came to get him."

"Where is John, now?"

CHAPTER 52

THE GIFT

"I think I'll let your young man speak for himself," Aunt Mary said, her cheeks flushed pink, her hands quivering. She darted out to the stairway.

"John, please come up here."

"Coming," John said.

Hannah's heart thrummed in her ears at the sound of his voice. She clutched at the bed linens with white-knuckled hands and hitched a breath.

John burst into the room, his cheeks ruddy and his brown hair windblown and disheveled.

To Hannah, he had never looked better. She grinned at him foolishly, speechless.

"Hannah," John said, his eyes lighting up. In two steps he was at her side, laughing, kissing her eyes, her face and her lips, as he cradled her in his arms.

Hannah clung to him, and in that moment nothing else mattered, nothing but the love shining in his eyes and the answering love swelling her heart.

Then she remembered. "I've done a terrible thing, John," she said. "I left the Two Sisters without the captain's permission. He's bound to have me put in jail for breaking my contract. I didn't know what else to do . . . I was only trying to get help for Pa." Ragged sobs tore at her throat.

"Hush," he said, caressing her cheek. "I stopped by the canal dock on our way here. I went on board the Two Sisters, looking for you.

Hannah lifted her head from John's chest. "Captain Bray must have been fit to be tied," she said, trembling. "Did he fire Seneca Joe and McIntyre because of me?"

John looked puzzled. "He didn't say anything about that. The only one he was mad at was you."

Hannah sniffled. "What's he going to do?"

"Well, he was going to have you arrested," said John, his eyes dancing, "until I bought the remainder of your contract, at what I suspect was a highly inflated price. Between my money and your confiscated salary, he shouldn't have any trouble hiring a new cook before he leaves Rome."

Hannah threw her arms around his neck. "I love you, John Nichols."

"Promise me I won't have to keep getting you out of trouble after we're married," John whispered against her ear.

Hannah laughed, grinning wickedly.

"I almost forgot," John said, "I brought you a present." He reached in his pocket.

Hannah blinked back tears of joy as John dangled her mother's gold locket before her eyes, then slipped the chain around her neck.

AUTHOR'S NOTE

I hope you have enjoyed this glimpse of nineteenth century life in a small village in the foothills of the Adirondacks and the bustling city of Rome – the birthplace of the Erie Canal.

Life in the 1860s was difficult and dangerous. With no known way to prevent cholera and typhoid fever, epidemics took the lives of many every summer.

The Erie Canal has been romanticized in books, movies and song, but it was hard and dangerous work. Canawlers, as they were sometimes called, were rough and rowdy men, often considered coarse and ill-mannered by those who stood higher on the social ladder. But these hard-working people, along with the mules who labored with them and the boats they sailed on, were the backbone of the Erie Canal and the bulwark of New York State's rise to economic greatness. I hope you come away with an appreciation for the work of those hardy men and women. The *Two Sisters* was a line boat out of Westernville with Captain Bray in command.

When Hannah's Pa was injured, he had to be left at a boarding house. Even if she had been allowed to stay with him, she would not have had enough money.

When my sister had emergency surgery in a hospital many miles from my home, I wanted to be with her. Hospital policy kept me from staying at the hospital, but, Sarah House, a hospitality house, was there for me. Sarah House provided comfortable home-like lodging, warm, caring volunteer staff, as well as transportation to and from the hospital each day – all for a small donation. In appreciation of their kindness, I will donate a portion of money from the sale of this book to Sarah House.

No book set in the mid 1860s can ignore the impact of the Civil War on everyday life. My great grandfather's letters to his wife in Boonville, showed me the thoughts and concerns of a local soldier. I have included excerpts from 1864 editions of the Black River Herald, including official dispatches from the Secretary of War and from officers in the field. The poem,

Mustered Out, appeared on the front page of the May 19th 1864 edition. If you want to know more about how the civil war was reported in this locality, the Black River Herald can be read on microfilm at the Erwin Library in Boonville.

I used many books in my research, among them: *Boonville and Its Neighbors,* by Tharratt G. Best; *Snubbing Posts: An Informal History of the Black River Canal,* by Thomas C. O'Donnell; *The Erie Canal: The Ditch that Opened a Nation,* by Dan Murphy; *The History of Oneida County;* and *Insurance Maps of Rome, Oneida County, New York,* which provided a street by street map of early Rome.

I acknowledge: the staff of the Rome Historical Society for assistance with research; the ideas and support of my writer's group – thanks, Jo Ann, Sue, Liana and Mary; and Susan and Rob, for their invaluable assistance. A special thank you to: Judy Routson, Boonville Herald Columnist and contributing writer; Mary Case, Middle Grade English Teacher; Merry K Speicher, Executive Director, Rome Historical Society,

PUBLISHER'S NOTE

This is the second Spruce Gulch Press book centered around the Erie Canal in the 1860s. We believe it is also an accurate reflection of life then. The working conditions Hannah faced on the Two Sisters were not unusual. Cooks were expected to provide food at any time it was wanted, and were typically always on call. She was not considered unusually young for such a job. Most people started working as adults in their early teens, usually in jobs found by their fathers. It's not an issue in this story, but, in most states the father was entitled to their child's wages until the child was twenty-one. The contract specifying pay at the end of the season was not at all unusual. People sold their labor and employers bought it with no supervision from any outside agency. The captain was right, the law would enforce her written agreement to stay on the boat until the season was over.

In those days, employers did not have a responsibility to provide care for employees injured on the job. There was also no workman's compensation or other governmental arrangement to help them. They paid for their own care, were aided by charity, or did without. By the mores of the time, her boss was being considerate in allowing Hannah to leave the boat to get her injured father settled. He was not unreasonable in not allowing her to leave the boat again.

The Erie Canal between Albany and the Great Lakes literally changed world history. Before the canal, Boston and Philadelphia were the financial and intellectual centers of the northern states. The canal gave both people and goods a way to move more quickly, at much less cost. It gave Upstate New York farmers a way to move their crops to market, changing them from subsistence farmers to prosperous agriculturalists. These factors combined to give New York City the dominance it has kept since then.

America also developed great civil engineers to build and operate the Erie Canal. It can fairly be credited with a major impact on education. The second generation of farmers the canal made prosperous were well educated and active in the great missions of their day, from the Transcendental Movement, to the Underground Railroad, to the Industrial Revolution. We too often forget that the canal itself was only a highway. It needed boats, with people to work on them and mules to pull them. The boat crew lived on the boats. They were people, good and bad, as we are today. The Two Sisters was a real boat, as were the names of several people. We have no way of knowing the actual personalities of these men and women. We believe we have described life on the Erie Canal as it was.

We found Hannah and The Two Sisters a good read, and are proud to publish it.